COPYRIGHT

Until Forever Comes
Copyright © 2013 Cardeno C.
Issued by: The Romance Authors, LLC, July, 2015
http://www.theromanceauthors.com

Print ISBN: 978-1-942184-38-6

Editor: Jae Ashley
Interior Book Design: Kelly Shorten
Cover Artist: Jay Aheer

DEDICATION

To Crissy Morris: For being a cheerleader, musical inspiration, and friend, thank you.

To Kelly Shorten: For all your help with web design, blog design, and everything else—thank you!

To Mary Calmes: I can't think of this book without remembering long nights chatting and laughing. Thank you for loving Miguel and Ethan right along with me.

CHAPTER 1

I'M going to confess that this here was not how I had seen the night going. Trapped in a dark—and, might I add, stinky—alley. Surrounded by bloodsuckers. Two pack mates in wolf form passed out against the wheel of a truck, not clear whether they were living or dead. The rest of our ragtag crew had already skedaddled, frantic to make it home so they could lick their wounds before they passed out. And the tall, fierce vampire responsible for fully half of the pummeling we'd taken still looked fit as a fiddle as he stalked toward me. His long black hair blew behind him while he swiped his hands on his shirt to remove shifter entrails, spit on the ground to ensure that the blood in his mouth wouldn't get absorbed into his system, and glared at me furiously.

"Ralph, don't," Scariest-of-Them-All growled at the bloodsucker that had me pinned against the rough brick. Blood oozed out the sides of my neck and both wrists in a steady flow, a puddle already forming around my feet, my heart finally, blessedly slowing.

Pinning-Me-To-The-Wall vampire, the one he called Ralph, held both of my wrists above my head with one hand and had just moved his free hand to my belly, claws at the ready, when the order to stop registered. He looked back over his shoulder, but didn't release me. Not that I could have gotten away even if he had loosened his grip. There were seven of them and one of me. Plus, they were bigger, stronger, older. I chuckled at the last thought. They were immortal; of course they were older.

Ralph jerked his head back and scowled as he shook me. "You think this is funny? Are you laughing, dog?" He spat the last word.

My head flopped from side to side, my neck feeling limp as a cooked noodle. Huh, I felt almost...almost good. I mean, I was bleeding like a stuck pig and dying and all, but dang. Everything inside was looser, easier, like I'd been suffocating all my life and I finally had room to breathe.

"You are," he said incredulously. "He is," he repeated for the benefit of the other vampires. He was using the same volume level, so I wasn't sure why it was necessary, but whatever. I shrugged, or at least I tried to shrug. I definitely shrugged in my mind. Could shrugs be mental? "Glad you think it's funny, because it's the last thing you're ever going to feel." He pressed his claws against my belly, cutting through my shirt and just piercing my skin. "Say goodbye, doggy."

"Ralph!" the vampire with the long black hair shouted. I wondered if his eyes were the same color as his hair. Mine were. The same color as his hair, I mean. Not the same color as mine. My hair was brown but my eyes were black. Black as night. Black as coal. Black as—"One more inch and I'll rip your head off myself!" Fiercer-Than-Them-All bloodsucker yelled at Ralph. "Step away from him."

Ralph shook me one last time and then let go. I slumped against the wall, barely able to stay on my feet. I wondered whether that was what being drunk felt like. I'd never been drunk. Maybe I should have tried it. Oh, well. Pretty soon, it wouldn't matter none anyhow. Nothing would matter ever again.

"Fine. You want the kill, Miguel, he's yours," Ralph said, and then he spit at me. It landed on my leg, I think, but there was so much blood it was nigh on impossible to tell. "I don't need any more of their poison on me anyway."

From the corner of my eye, I could see my previously prone pack mates moving. They were alive. With the bloodsuckers staring at their comrade approaching his next victim (uh, that was me, in case it wasn't clear), Harold and George were able to drag themselves away. Good.

I turned my attention back to the threat slash salvation at hand. Coming at me in slow, steady footsteps was Miguel, the scary vampire who had maimed most of my pack mates and was apparently gunning to add me to his accomplishment tally, the one with the gorgeous long black hair and the—Wait, gorgeous? How much blood had I lost? Enough that death was imminent. Not that I minded.

That was, after all, the whole reason I had agreed to go on the vampire-eradication mission with the other males my age. Hell, it was the reason they had, for the first time since we were toddlers, let me join them for anything.

An unarmed shifter who couldn't shift wouldn't

survive a confrontation with a coven of bloodsuckers. We all knew that going in. The others were there to defend the pack from our most detested enemy and gain notoriety for years to come. Me? I was there to die in the only honorable way my twenty-year-old brain could think of.

But like I said, things didn't turn out like I'd expected. Because the closer that bloodsucker named Miguel got to me, the more I felt blood pooling somewhere other than around my shoes. My pants weren't tight, but, unlike the rest of my body, my prick wasn't small, and in its erect state, it didn't have enough room to hide. I wondered if their kind could see well at night. Probably. They were nocturnal, like our wolves, so if they couldn't see well in the dark, they wouldn't be able to hunt, wouldn't be able to feed. Oh, Lord, *feed*.

What would that feel like? I stared at Tall, Dark, and Deadly and wondered how it would feel to have those sharp fangs pierce my vein and suck the blood from my body. My knees buckled at the thought. The vampire's gaze met mine. He licked his lips and that was it. Endgame. I was done, twitching and gasping as I coated the inside of my drawers with my release.

His eyes widened in surprise and his graceful steps faltered. Sure enough, they could see in the dark. Or maybe they had a heightened sense of smell.

Miguel got even closer, and I was finally able to track his scent over the millions of other foreign odors in the filthy half-soul street. I trembled with renewed desire.

No. Couldn't be. Not possible.

He took another step. And then another one. His gaze never broke its lock on mine.

My eyes rolled back in my head, the tightness in my skin completely loosened. The pressure in my chest slowed to nonexistent. And then I was on all fours, peace finally overtaking me, before everything went black.

CHAPTER 2

IT WAS light outside when I woke. Huh, I reckoned I wasn't dead after all. I took in a deep breath and sighed in disappointment. I couldn't even manage to die right.

"Ethan?"

Was that my sister's voice calling to me?

"Ethan?"

She sounded panicked.

"Ethan! Are you out here?"

Out here? Out where? I blinked and looked around. I was alone in the same dingy alley from the previous night.

"Please, please, you have to be here. You just have to... Ethan!" she screamed.

Yeah, I was there. The question was, what was Crissy doing there? A female shouldn't be off pack lands at all, let alone by herself. Not that I was following the rules any better. At twenty, I had no right leaving pack lands either. None of us should have been out there. But my pack mates had been looking for glory. And I had been looking for... I sighed again. I had been looking for something I'd never find. There was no honor in a shifter who couldn't shift. Not even an honorable death, apparently. Why hadn't the bloodsuckers killed me?

I climbed to my feet, ready to respond to my sister's cries, when I noticed that my perception was catawampus. Everything seemed higher...or I seemed shorter. I mean, I wasn't a big guy on my best day, but this was... Were those paws? I lifted my right hand, and sure enough, that there was a paw. A quick check of my left showed the same situation. I had paws. That meant I had shifted, right? I'd shifted!

If I had been in my human form, I would have cried from the joy of it. I was happier than a puppy with two peters, so I started yipping and hopping toward Crissy's voice. She was going to be so proud of me. My whole family would, of course. It'd been hard on them, I knew, having a cub who had never shifted, who could barely run without passing out, who was weaker at twenty than he had been at eight. But they'd stood by me, finding pleased looks to send my way and words of praise for whatever insignificant accomplishment I'd mustered.

My sister was different, though. Her expressions were never forced, her pride never put-on. She had always loved me just as I was. So much so that she had made me find a way to love myself.

"Ethan? Is that you?" Crissy was staring at me, wide-eyed. I ran to her and jumped up, hitting her thighs with my paws. "Oh praise the Lord, it is. Ethan, you—" Her eyes were suddenly wet. "You shifted." She plopped down on the ground, right there in that filthy alley, not caring that her long flowered skirt was going to get stained, and wrapped her arms around my neck, her tears dripping onto my fur.

My fur. God, it felt weird to think it. I had fur! Finally.

"When you didn't come home last night, we was so scared, and then those no 'count fools confessed what y'all had done. They said you was de—" She shook her head. "Doesn't matter what they said. Look at you! You're a wolf. A beautiful brown wolf."

She petted my flank and I licked her face. My tail was wagging like one of those dogs the bloodsucker had accused me of being. I didn't care one bit. Something had finally gone right. *I* was finally right.

"Let's go home. Mama and Pop are fit to be tied. They're talkin' to the Alpha now, gettin' permission to put together a search party."

We both knew they'd still be trying to get that permission when we got home. The Alpha wasn't going to take up anyone's time to look for me. He was probably dancing a jig thinking I was finally gone. After all, a pack was only as strong as its weakest member, and I'd been considered the weak link since puberty hit and I still hadn't shifted. But all that had changed now. I would no longer be a source of shame for my family. The relief was freeing beyond anything I'd known.

"I don't know what all y'all were thinkin', Ethan," my sister said as we started the long trek out of Kfarkattan and back to the woods that held our home. "Sneakin' away at night to go to townie bars."

I wasn't surprised the other guys had lied to the pack about what we'd been doing. Going into town to go to bars and being attacked by vampires was one thing. If the elders knew we'd searched out the bloodsuckers and instigated the fight, we'd all be in line for a whupping from our folks.

"When I was your age, we used to have boondockers in the woods," Crissy continued her lecture. "Next time y'all want to drink, let me know. I'll buy some beer and y'all can stay on pack lands to drink it. Nobody has to know." She shook her head. "Comin' to the bars in Kfarkattan is right dangerous. Especially now with all them bloodsuckers around. Y'all are lucky they didn't kill you."

True enough. I'd never felt more lucky. After all, I could shift now. And I didn't hurt. My heart no longer felt like it was too big for my chest. My skin no longer ached like it had been stretched too tight. Even the scabs from where the bloodsucker had clawed me didn't bother me all that much. I assumed the shift had helped speed up the healing. Yup, I was one lucky shifter.

The walk home took two hours, same as the walk into town. But on the way there, I'd barely kept up with the other boys. My heart had been pounding in my chest. My swollen limbs had protested every movement. Now, though? Now I was trotting alongside my sister, enjoying the feel of the cool morning breeze ruffling my fur and blowing against my snout.

Crissy had been quiet for a while, so I glanced up and saw her looking down at me with wet eyes. "I'm happy for you, Ethan." She wiped her hand across the corner of her eye. "Not because there was anythin' wrong with you before, mind," she added firmly. "But because I know how much you wanted—" She paused, presumably trying to come up with the right words to finish that sentence: how much I wanted to be normal, how much I wanted to stop being a stress to my family, how much I wanted to stop shaming my pack. "How much you wanted to fit in, how much you dislike being different."

I rubbed my head against her leg in a loving gesture, and she reached down and tangled her fingers in my scruff. We walked together in silence. She reached down and petted me every so often. It was peaceful, just the two of us together, and I remembered that even before I'd shifted, I'd been lucky for at least one reason: I had Crissy for a sister. We were deep in the woods, steps away from our parents' den, when she spoke again.

"Just remember, little brother, whatever happens, different ain't bad." She stopped walking, so I halted too, and tilted my head to the side, looking up at her in question. "You're special, Ethan." She said the words I'd heard from her lips countless times during my childhood. "Those other boys are fine. If you want to be friends with them, that's okay. Just remember, they're here now, but they'll be in the past soon enough. Friends will come and go every time the sun rises and sets. Kin too. All of us will be gone. Except for you. You—" She pulled in a deep breath and let it out slowly, and then she looked at me in that unique way she had, the way where her eyes became almost cloudy and it seemed like she was looking at something else, something the rest of us couldn't see, that way my parents and her husband had told her never to do outside of our home. A cold chill washed over me, like someone done walked over my grave. "You're special, Ethan Abbatt. You'll save us all."

We stood still. The familiar background noises in the forest—the birds, the wind, the rustling leaves—all of it disappeared. I looked at my sister, not understanding what her words meant. She looked through me, as if she could see more than any shifter.

Eventually she blinked and her eyes cleared, the thickness in the air dissipated, and familiar sounds surrounded us once again.

"I'm pregnant," she said. If I had been in my human form, I would have hugged her. As it was, I yipped quietly. "Twins. These here are girls," she added as she rubbed her hand over her belly and started walking again.

Five boys in six years. Her husband had been proud after the first one. He had strutted like a peacock after the second. After the third, he had laughed somewhat uncomfortably at the comments from his friends about his virility and masculinity. By the time the fourth had been born, Richie looked nervous and tired. I'd even overheard him telling my sister they needed to stop or at least slow down. When we were waiting in his living room while the midwife and my mama helped my sister deliver the fifth, he said a prayer that should have been too quiet for me to hear, but somehow the words had drifted over and surprised me.

"Please, Lord," he'd begged. "Please give her a daughter."

I'd never heard a male ask for a daughter. Sons meant strength to build homes and hunt for food, power for the pack, and warriors to fight against the bloodsuckers and shield us from the humans, or half-souls, as the pack called them. My fifth nephew had entered the world ten minutes later, healthy and pink and chubby, just like his brothers.

"Richie doesn't believe me," my sister said with a chuckle. "Not that he says that, mind. He just smiles and nods, but I know he thinks we're having another boy. He's wrong, though." She dropped down to the ground and grinned brightly. I stopped walking. "We're finally gettin' our girls," she whispered. And then she threw her arms around me and squeezed tightly, the hug feeling familiar even though my body wasn't.

"Crissy?" Richie's voice rang out. "Is that you?"

"Right here, Richie," my sister responded as she stood.

The door to my parents' house slammed, as if he'd let it go without taking the time to close it. I heard his heavy, fast footsteps and knew he was running toward us.

"Oh, Lord, Criss!" he shouted in relief as he reached us and pulled his wife into his arms, not seeming to notice me on the ground. "Darlin', where you been? With everythin' happenin' with your brother, I reckoned you'd be helpin' your kin. When your folks done said they hadn't seen you in hours, I near about lost my mind."

She stood on tiptoe and kissed his cheek as she patted his chest. "I *was* helpin'. I went to find Ethan."

"You"—he bowed up and narrowed his eyes

dangerously—"you what, now?"

Not intimidated in the least, despite her husband's significant height and weight advantage, my sister giggled. "I done brought my brother home." She cocked her head and moved her gaze toward me.

"Are you sayin' you went into town?" Richie raised his voice, something he rarely did when speaking to his wife. He tore his ever-present straw cowboy hat off his head and slammed it against his thigh. "Damn it all to hell, Crissy, that's right dangerous. What in tarnation was you thinkin' wanderin' off pack lands?"

"Well..." She drew the word out slowly and moved her gaze from her husband to me again. "I figured I'd collect Ethan and bring him on home."

He finally followed her gaze and saw me sitting on the ground in wolf form. I yipped and raised my paw, then scratched at his knee.

"Well, boy howdy, how about that!" His anger disappeared at the sight of my wolf, and he bent down and patted my head. "Way to go, Ethan! We knew you could do it."

No, they hadn't. Hoped, sure enough. But knew? Nope. At twenty, I was a good decade older than even the slowest male shifter was when he first took wolf form. Nobody, not even me, had expected me to be able to shift by that point. And because I got weaker year after year, I was pretty sure they all expected me to pass young. Well, all of them except Crissy.

Thinking of my sister's unwavering loyalty and support

had me changing back into my human form. I wrapped my arms around her and pulled her close, resting my forehead against hers. We were the same height, not because Crissy was particularly tall, but because I was knee-high to a grasshopper. She'd always told me that made me the perfect height to hug. I blinked tears out of my eyes as I thought of that and held her tight.

"Thank you," I whispered roughly.

She patted my back.

"All right, y'all. I think that there's enough of that. Ethan, I'm proud of you, now shoo." Richie waved his hat toward my folks' house. "Go on and get some clothes on."

I chuckled as I pulled back from my sister's arms and punched him in the shoulder. "You jealous, Richie?"

He shrugged and tugged on my sister's arm until she was pressed against his side, then he draped his arm over her shoulders possessively. "Call me old-fashioned, but I don't enjoy seein' a man touchin' my wife, and a naked one at that. Now get! Your folks are inside wearin' a hole in the floor."

"She's my sister!" I shouted with a laugh. "That's just nasty." But I walked away with a strut in my step. No one had ever called me a man; no one had ever seen me as a threat to anything.

"That was nice of you," I heard my sister whisper to her husband just as I moseyed into the house.

"Richie?" my mama called out as soon as I opened the squeaky door.

"No, it's me, Mama," I answered.

"Ethan!" She rushed out of the kitchen, wiping her hands on a towel before throwing her arms around me and rocking from side to side. "Oh, my baby, my baby."

"I'm okay, Mama," I said. "Honest."

She sniffled and nodded as she moved back and cupped my face between her moist palms. "Sure enough. Such a strong boy." She took in a deep breath and then looked back over her shoulder and raised her voice. "Gerald, our boy's home."

My father hustled over, his brow furrowed, concern etched all over his face.

"Sorry I worried you, Pop," I said quietly as I lowered my eyes.

"Well"—he cleared his throat—"I reckon there's no real harm done seein' as how you're hale and healthy. You're gettin' older, and it's natural for you to push, Ethan. And I know you spend a lot of time on your lonesome, so I was right happy to hear that you was running about with some other boys." He paused and waited for me to look up and meet his gaze before continuing. "But you worried your mama something fierce layin' out all night with no word. We can't have that again."

"I'm sorry, Mama," I said, and she hugged me again, still sniffling.

"Uh, son," my father said hesitantly. "Why're you in the altogether? Where're your clothes?"

I gave my mama a final squeeze and stepped back.

"I've got news," I said quietly. Then with a deep breath, I crouched down and called my wolf, feeling my body change until I was standing on all fours, and then looked up at my astonished parents.

My father was first to break the silence. "Well, I'll be," he said, his voice cracking.

"Oh, my," my mama added, tears streaming freely down her face. "Would you look at that."

CHAPTER 3

BY MIDDAY my arms were throbbing a fair bit and my chest felt like it was just on the wrong side of tight, but I chalked it up to the shifting. After all, those bones changing and moving was something foreign to me, so it made sense I'd be sore after. It seemed odd that the pain got worse, instead of better, as the day went on, but I ignored it. I'd hurt more than that for as long as I could remember, so if my heart was beating a tad faster than it had in the morning and my skin felt a smidge tighter, well, I reckoned I was still doing all right.

But then the strangest thing happened. I was outside, taking a little walk after supper in the hope it would ease the tightness in my legs so I could go to sleep, when the image of that black-haired bloodsucker's face popped into my head. I remembered meeting his gaze and wishing I could see the color of his eyes in the dark. I remembered his long, lean frame gliding toward me. I remembered my body's reaction to him, to the thought of his fangs piercing my skin and drawing out my blood. I shuddered and the throbbing in my veins intensified.

What was wrong with me? That vampire and his

buddies had been planning to kill me and I was getting turned on by the memory? Apparently, being able to shift didn't mean I was no longer weird.

I shook off the unwelcome thoughts about long hair and a strong body and kept walking, trying to focus on the beauty of the sunlight filtering in through the trees and the familiar scents of pine and earth. I failed on both counts, because all I could think about was the beauty of the strong warrior as his hair flowed behind him when he flew at me, and the scent of his skin, spicy and warm, like cinnamon and cloves. It had instantly brought my pecker to attention in the alley, and I was having the same reaction in response to the memory. But it wasn't only my prick that throbbed: all my veins pulsed with blood, and I wanted more than anything to have the vampire suck me and release the pressure.

Super. I was just coming out of my run as the pack freak because I was the only male shifter in memory who'd been unable to take his wolf form by so late in life and because I was smaller than the other males, and because I was weaker than, well, it seemed like I was weaker than everyone and... Wait. Where was I going with this uplifting internal monologue?

I couldn't remember what I'd been thinking or doing. My body just moved, seemingly of its own accord. And suddenly I was surprised to find myself in town alone, the sky completely black. Had I walked there? I was having trouble concentrating on anything except the pounding in my veins. I clung to a thread of clarity in my head that said I didn't belong on that street, surrounded by half-soul shops and houses.

Deciding that I needed to shift and run home, I ducked into an alley and stripped out of my clothes. But when I called my wolf form, nothing happened. Or rather, I couldn't shift, but something did happen. The dull ache I'd been enduring turned into a pain so sharp it stole my breath. I felt too full, like my body was carrying more than it should, like my heart and my veins and my skin were going to explode. I collapsed onto the ground and curled into a ball, trying to catch my breath.

And that was when I heard him.

"I'm hungry," my vampire growled. *My vampire.* Even in my foggy mental state, I knew something wasn't right about that thought, but I couldn't put my finger on it.

"You've been feeding all night, Miguel. This one is your third, and you've already drained him more than you should. Let's go."

"Hungry," Miguel's deep voice rumbled. And then I heard a frightened scream.

"If you take any more, you'll kill him, and we don't need that kind of attention. This town isn't as big as what we're used to. Besides, you can't still be hungry. Let's go."

I crawled on forearms and knees, body held low to the ground, and peeked around the corner. Miguel had a pale, trembling half-soul pinned to the wall, two unconscious males lay at his feet, and another vampire stood next to him, his hand on Miguel's shoulder, seemingly trying to restrain him.

My arms and knees felt damp. I lifted one arm at a time in front of my face and turned them. Red, slick, warm. I was bleeding. When I lowered my gaze to my legs, I saw blood drizzling there too. It looked as if I had been dragged over gravel, probably because I'd been dragging myself over exactly that. Sharp rocks and glass had pierced my skin, and my veins were happy at the opportunity to release their burden. I kept crawling forward, looking down at the ground so I might could avoid any more damage.

"I'm hungry," Miguel rumbled again, and I returned my focus to him. He dipped his face toward the man's neck and opened his mouth. I barked.

Barked? I shook my head and looked down to see my bloody skin had been replaced by fur. When had I shifted?

I wasn't the only one surprised by my bark. Miguel and the other vampires turned their heads in my direction. The half-soul stayed as he was: crying and shaking. The stench of urine told me he had soiled himself.

I walked over to them, no thought, no plan, just an uncontrollable need to keep the bloodsucker away from that man. I didn't want Miguel touching him, feeding from him. So much so that I growled at the mere possibility. And it wasn't because I wanted to protect the frightened half-soul.

"What the hell?" the vampire who wasn't Miguel said as he stared at me. "More dogs? I would've thought the ones last night would've gone home and warned the rest of the mutts to stay where they belong." He shook his head and sneered. "There was no point in letting them live. Damn dogs can't seem to understand their place." He took a step toward me. "Well, I'm sure as fuck not making that mistake again."

Miguel let go of the half-soul and reached for his comrade, preventing him from moving closer to me. Without the vampire holding him up, the half-soul slid down the wall and sat on the ground, gasping as tears streamed down his face.

"You deal with the humans," Miguel ordered the other vampire. "I'll take care of the wolf."

The vampire ran a disdainful gaze over the three half-souls collapsed on the ground. "Deal with the humans?" he asked.

"Yes. You said we don't need the attention, right? They were all drunk before we fed. Take them to their homes, and by morning, they won't remember any of this. And if they do"—Miguel shrugged—"they'll think it was all a dream."

Looked more like a nightmare to me, but I wasn't in any form to comment. Literally.

"*We* didn't feed," the vampire grumbled. "*You* fed. And you didn't share."

Faster than my eyes could follow, Miguel backhanded the other vampire, sending him flying several feet until he slammed against a parked truck. Blood dripped from his nose and lip. He licked his upper lip and wiped a hand across his face, smearing a streak of red over it. Though he didn't roll over and show his belly, the vampire did as he was told. He climbed to his feet and, with slumped shoulders, approached the human male Miguel had released, who was now just as passed out as his friends.

If I hadn't already felt the power rolling off Miguel, the interaction I was witnessing would have told me who was Alpha. Or the vampire version of Alpha. I had no idea what they called their leaders. Regardless of his title, this was the vampire who was staying behind to *take care* of me. Those had been Miguel's words, right?

I should have been terrified.

I should have fled.

My whole life, I'd been warned about the bloodsuckers. They had no souls, no values, no respect for nature or community or family. And while my kind limited interaction with the half-souls as a general rule, we didn't abuse them. They were weaker than shifters and we didn't prey on the weak, a concept the bloodsuckers didn't understand. The one in front of me, Miguel, looked to be the worst of their kind, hurting and terrifying defenseless half-souls without mercy.

But despite all that, I didn't move when the not-Miguel-vampire roughly snatched the unconscious half-soul off the ground and moved away with the male in tow.

I didn't move when the Miguel-vampire stood straight and tall and turned his sharp, piercing gaze on me.

And I didn't move when, after the other vampire and the half-soul were gone, Miguel started walking—*was he gliding?*—toward me.

I looked at his feet, happy to see them touching the

ground, and then I looked at his face, happy to see he'd focused completely on me. I sat up and tried to smile, which was difficult in wolf form and incredibly stupid in I-was-about-to-get-my-hide-tanned form. I was pretty sure my tail was moving from side to side. I refused to even *think* of it as wagging.

"I expected you to return to your kind, wolf," Miguel said, his voice, strong but quiet, coming from barely parted lips. "I came to check on yo—" He stopped mid-word, looking surprised by what he'd said. "I walked by that alley after sundown and you were gone, but I could smell another wolf. A female who smelled like you, but...didn't. I thought she'd come to collect you."

Vampires could scent? That was something I hadn't known. And for him to have distinguished the connection in scents between me and Crissy meant the bloodsuckers' sense of smell was just as sophisticated as ours.

"Confused you, did I?" Miguel chuckled and grinned, looking pleased with himself.

I wondered if he could read my mind, if that was another vampire trait of which I'd been unaware. But then I realized my head was tipped to the side, my brow furrowed, and I reckoned that being able to read body language would have been enough for him to sense what I was thinking.

Of course, to be able read my body language, the vampire had to be looking at my body. I straightened my posture at the realization. And I felt something else getting straighter too, or rather it was getting harder, which meant it wasn't really straight. It curved and veered right, actually.

"Well, you confuse me too, wolf." Miguel's voice was suddenly huskier and he was near about close enough to touch. "You smell...different." He took in a deep breath through his nose and shuddered. "You smell *good*."

I got up and took the two steps necessary to reach him, then stretched my neck up and nudged his crotch with my snout. He made a noise that was part laugh, part groan. Then he put his hand on my head and pushed me back.

"Doesn't matter how good you smell. I'm not sticking my dick in an animal. *Shift*." He palmed his groin, and I saw what looked to be a nice-sized bulge filling his jeans. "I've wanted to fuck your skinny ass since you came in your pants last night."

Fuck my ass? I froze, an image of what he described in my mind: me in human form, naked on all fours, him behind me, pushing into my body. I'd seen pack members tie in wolf form. I'd even managed to spy some of them nude and writhing together in human form on the forest floor, under the moon. But I'd never seen two males together.

Male shifters tied with female shifters. It was the only way for a female to release her wolf and the only way for a male to maintain his humanity. Each shifter's soul shared two forms, two bodies: a wolf and a human. Females' souls favored the human form, while males' souls favored the wolf. In order for a female to shift, she had to accept a tie from a male wolf. For that reason, females shifted later in life. Males, on other hand, shifted as cubs, but their connection to their human half weakened as they aged, and they needed to tie with a female shifter in order to hang on to their humanity.

I hadn't expected to tie with anybody, ever. I mean, I hadn't ever been able to shift into my wolf, so how could I help a female connect with hers? Plus, I hadn't figured on living much into my adulthood. My family had endured looks of pity and disgust from pack members as a result of my inability to shift. Though they'd tried to shield me, I'd heard the words: sick, wrong, abomination, better off dead.

Although I was now able to shift, my newly developing attraction to a male vampire was sure to make the comments about me worse. The whole basis of shifter society was rooted in the concept of the connection between males and females, in the need to tie. So there was no question in my mind about how the elders would react if they knew what I was feeling: they'd say two males together was wrong. They'd say being with a vampire was worse. My parents would probably say it too. Maybe even my sister.

But it didn't feel wrong. Not in my head, not in my heart, and not in the rest of my body. In fact, nothing had ever felt more right than being in Miguel's presence or thinking about being held in his strong arms. So I closed my eyes and called to my human.

"There you are," Miguel said, caressing my head with his big cool hand. I blinked up at him. "You're shivering. Do you have clothes, young one, or did you come out here in your wolf form?"

I frowned as I rose to my feet. "I'm twenty. I'm not

young." I crossed my arms over my chest. "I'm a man."

One side of Miguel's mouth turned up and he twitched his lips in amusement. It was the first smile I'd seen on his face that didn't look predatory. "Twenty, you say? I'm more than four hundred years old." He dropped his gaze between my legs and then the increasingly familiar and arousing wicked grin spread across his face. "But you are most definitely a man. Who would've thought such a small body would have such a big dick?"

I blushed at his crude words and instinctively tried to cover myself with my hands.

Miguel groaned and then licked my cheek, from my jaw to just under my eye, over and over again. It was such a canine gesture that it took me off guard.

"I can see your blood just beneath your skin." His voice was husky and low. "I can hear it." He licked his lips.

"Hear it?" I whispered.

"Your blood. I can hear your blood thrumming through your veins. It's so loud." He dipped his head and grazed my neck with an open mouth. "Never heard it so strongly before. It's like it's calling to me."

With no thought toward self-preservation, I cocked my head and offered my neck to the bloodsucker, whom I had just witnessed all but killing a man. And that was after he'd drained two other half-souls who were, at that moment, still lying on the ground not more than fifteen feet from us.

"I can't drink you, wolf," he said regretfully as he continued mouthing my skin. "Your kind is poison, not food."

I knew that, of course. The fact that vampires were allergic to shifter blood was one of our strengths during battle. Without the ability to suck us dry, they lost their primary tool and we were more evenly matched.

Despite that, I needed Miguel to feed from me. Not because I wanted to hurt him, but because I could feel what he described too. Not thirty minutes had passed since I'd crouched on the ground, bleeding, but already my body felt too full, my skin too tight. It was a familiar feeling, one I'd lived with for as long as I could remember. But only in that moment did I recognize it for what it was: too much blood in my body, in my veins, in my heart. I needed release, and I knew instinctively that Miguel could give it to me.

"So warm," he said as he licked and kissed the pulsing veins in my neck. I trembled, and he pulled his face back, pursing his lips in disapproval. "And we need to make sure you stay that way. You need to shift back or we need to find you something to wear, and then I'll walk you out of town."

"But I...I," I stammered. "I thought you were going to... thought we were fixin' to..." I could feel my neck and face heating even more. I didn't have the words to finish that sentence. I just knew I wanted something, needed something, felt as if I'd die if I didn't get...something.

Miguel wrapped his arms around me and pulled me right up against him. "So shy," he whispered and gazed at me. "I'd forgotten what that was like."

"What do you mean?" I asked as I burrowed closer to him, moving my hands up his sides and clinging to his shirt.

"I haven't been with someone so new in years." He rubbed my lower back as he skated his lips over my jaw. "Decades." He reached my mouth, and my entire body shook with need, my heart slammed against my ribs, and my breath came out in short, desperate gasps. He paused, and then he looked into my eyes. "Have you ever been kissed?"

I shook my head.

"Centuries," he said so quietly that I felt more than heard the words. Then he cupped my cheeks between his hands, cocked my head up, dipped his face, and touched his lips to mine.

CHAPTER 4

I WAS standing in Kfarkattan, not wearing any clothing, being held by a vampire. That should sound like a nightmare of the most terrifying variety. But I wasn't scared. Not with Miguel caressing my face, tracing his thumbs over my jaw, opening and closing his lips over mine in barely there, gentle tugs, darting his tongue out and lapping at mine every so often.

Necking with a soulless killer wasn't what I would have expected. He was tender and gentle, his gaze warm and full of desire, his body hard and muscular and nothing short of perfect. I melted against him, and he moaned, increasing the pressure of his lips against mine and sucking on my tongue.

"Ungh, ungh," I groaned and pushed my groin against him, looking for friction.

"So young," he said quietly and caressed my cheek as he gazed at me. "So innocent."

I saw something cross his expression then, something other than lust and desire, something closer to disappointment or sadness. But I couldn't think too long on it because suddenly he was kissing me again as he pressed his knee between my thighs, giving me something to rub on. Instinct took over, and I frantically rutted against him, grasping at his shirt, pouring my moans and whimpers into his mouth. And then I was shaking and coming and crying out his name.

When I came back to earth, I was still in Miguel's arms, snug as a bug, surrounded by his strength as he kissed and sucked on my neck. "You said my name," I heard him whisper. Then he pulled back and put his hands on my shoulders, holding me in place. His gaze bore into me. "How did you know my name?"

"I heard your, uh, friend say it. Is that…is that okay?"

"Yes." He nodded. "I like hearing my name from your lips. But I don't know what you're called."

"Ethan," I answered. "Ethan Abbatt."

"Ethan Abbatt." He repeated my name, sounding almost wistful as he said it. "I think it's time we got you home, Ethan Abbatt."

"What if I don't want to go?" I asked, hoping I didn't sound like a petulant child fixin' to pitch a fit.

He sighed and caressed my cheek, his gentleness once again surprising me. "You don't belong here, wolf. It isn't safe."

"But you're here," I responded.

He graced me with another of those crooked grins, the kind that made me feel like he thought I was amusing. I sensed that Miguel wasn't amused very often, so I felt proud that I could put that expression on his face, no matter the reason.

"Yes, I'm here for now. But I'm not a little wolf who

can't seem to stay out of trouble."

He had managed to say the one thing that was sure to tear me up right quick. I frowned and dropped my gaze. "I know I'm a runt, but I can't help my size," I said quietly.

"Hey." He tipped my chin up and forced me to meet his gaze. "It wasn't an insult. In case you hadn't noticed, I like how you look."

"Yeah?" I croaked, my voice breaking on the word.

"Oh, yeah." He dragged a heated gaze over every inch of my body and brought his hand along for the ride.

When he ended at my cheek, I turned my face and nuzzled his hand. "Good," I said.

"Yes, it is good. So good, in fact, that I want to make sure you keep on looking like this, except maybe without all those scrapes and cuts." He furrowed his brow and stared at my legs and arms. "Those aren't wounds from my kind, so they're not from last night." Suddenly all the humor left his face and he looked just as deadly as he had during the battle the night before. "Who hurt you?"

I looked down at my body and saw that while the abrasions from crawling on the ground had stopped bleeding and started healing when I shifted, they were still readily apparent.

"Nobody. It happened when I crawled to you."

"Crawled? Do you mean when you walked over in your wolf form?"

"No." I shook my head. "I heard you and I tried to shift but I couldn't, so I crawled and the ground was sharp and hard and it hurt when it cut into me, and I started bleeding, but then I was able to call my wolf and that's when I saw you and it didn't hurt no more."

Miguel furrowed his brow, looking like he was perplexed by what I'd said. Then he flicked his gaze all about and wrapped his arm around me, pulling me close. "Come on, wolf. Ted will be back any minute to get the other humans, and he might not be alone. You said you started out in your human form, right? That means you have clothes. Where are they?"

I opened my mouth to protest any plan that would ultimately lead to being forced away from him, but he narrowed his eyes, and something told me if I didn't answer his question, he'd get right ornery lickety-split. I much preferred a happy expression on Miguel's face, so I slumped my shoulders in defeat and cocked my chin toward the alley where I'd left my clothes.

"They're right over yonder," I answered.

He walked us over without another word, but he kept his arm around me, holding me close. I liked it.

When we got to my clothes, he fetched them and handed me my shirt. "Get dressed," he ordered.

I reached for my shirt and pulled it on. My socks came next. I hopped on each leg in turn to tug them on, feeling my pecker flopping from side to side, and heard a new sound—Miguel laughing.

"What?" I asked him.

He leaned down and kissed me. "You are by far the

most charming creature I have ever had the good fortune of encountering."

"Charming?"

A hot, dark gaze scanned my body yet again, from face to feet and back up. I was wearing a long-sleeved shirt and socks. Nothing else.

"Yeah," he said, his voice husky. "I'm feeling pretty *charmed* from watching you jump around with your stuff hanging out there." He cupped my package with his large hand and gave me a light squeeze. "And it is *really* nice-looking stuff. Almost a shame to cover up a dick this pretty."

"Then don't," I said.

"We can't walk you through town like this." Miguel chuckled. "Humans might be oblivious to some things, but a man without pants isn't one of them."

"Then we won't go through town," I suggested, realizing my voice sounded somewhat desperate. "You live here, right? Can't we go to your den?"

"My *den*?" Miguel repeated my question.

I nodded.

He looked at me suspiciously. "Why?" he asked.

Thinking he was worried I'd harm him if he let me into his private domain, I tried to relieve his fears. "I won't hurt you," I promised. "Or do anything to your den."

The no-longer-foreign laugh rolled out of him again. He shook out my drawers and held them out in front of me. "Get dressed, killer," he said.

I put one foot and then the other through the underwear.

"Are you making fun of me?" I asked with a frown.

He pulled them up until they rested at my waist. "No, never," he responded sarcastically.

"Yes, you are." I adjusted my genitals. "You're laughing at me," I said with my hand still in my drawers. "What's so funny?"

His smile took over his face and transformed it from frightening to adoring.

"Look, don't get all ruffled again." He held my cut-off jean shorts up. I pulled my hand away from my groin and put it over his hand so I could keep steady as I stepped into them. "But I found it just a tad amusing to hear you reassure me about my safety in your presence."

I crossed my arms over my chest. "Are you saying I'm weak?" I demanded. He pulled my cut-offs up and then zipped and buttoned them.

"No. I'm saying..." He hesitated, seeming to choose his words carefully as he crouched down on the ground and slipped each of my shoes on. "You're an innocent. I can see that. It isn't a bad thing. In fact, it's a great thing. But we need to get you back where you belong so you can stay that way."

"I am right where I belong, and I'm fixin' to stay here."

Miguel stood up and glanced around. "You belong in an alley in the middle of town with some injured humans down the way and an irritated vampire heading back any minute to get rid of them?" He shook his head. "I don't think so, wolf."

"I belong with you. If that's"—I waved my hands around—"this here alley, then that's where I'll be."

I reckoned he was about to tell me that dog wouldn't hunt so I tried to look as serious and strong as possible. Have you ever tried to *look* strong? Turned out it wasn't such an easy feat to accomplish. Seemed a certain pose wasn't quite enough to cut it. Either that or I didn't know the particular pose to strike.

"You belong where?" Miguel asked, looking perplexed.

"I belong with you," I repeated, trying to keep my voice from shaking. I was pretty sure I failed.

"I'm a vampire," he said, stating the obvious.

"I'm aware," I said.

He furrowed his brow. "You're a shifter." Again with the obvious.

"I surely know that too."

"Look, if you want me to take you to my place for a little fun, I can do that. But I'm trying to spare you here."

"Spare me?" I asked.

He nodded. "Yes, spare you. How do you think your pack will take it if you come home smelling of a vampire? You already smell like sex, but the scent is just your own, so they'll dismiss that as you having a bit of personal fun. If we—"

"I smell like sex?" I asked nervously, lifting my arms and sniffing them before poking my nose into my underarms.

Miguel moved my arms down to my sides. "Your pits aren't where you got your seed, wolf. But don't worry, like I said, right now it's just your seed. If I fuck you, you're going to be smelling of me for some time. No way to hide that. How do you think your pack would react to that?"

I gulped and tried not to shake. "It wouldn't be good," I admitted. "We're not supposed to diddle ourselves. And I haven't ever...well, there was the one time, just to see what it was like, but I don't diddle myself, and if—"

"*Diddle* yourself?" Miguel repeated incredulously. He shook his head and grasped my arm, then tugged me out of the alley. "You need to go home," he said. "You don't belong here."

"I am home," I insisted, dragging my feet in a failed attempt to slow him down. Damn, he was strong. "I'm staying with you. That's how things are supposed to be."

"Supposed to—" He shook his head again and kept walking. "You just said 'diddle.' Hell, you just said you *don't* diddle. You seem to have no idea how dangerous it is for you here. You seem to have no idea how dangerous *I* am, wolf. I am nobody's home."

But he was wrong. Wrong about all of it. He was my home. I knew it. There was no way to mistake his scent. No way to mistake the way my body reacted to him. Miguel was my mate. My true mate.

Some of the guys at school used to say there was no such thing, that true mates were a fairy tale. But I'd met a pair once, when we were visiting kin in another pack. And I'd heard tell about another pair my parents knew when they were young. So I knew true mates were real. I just hadn't expected to have one. Why would a broken shifter be bestowed with the greatest gift possible? But for whatever reason, I'd been blessed. I was about to explain that to Miguel when we heard a commotion.

"Who are you?" an angry voice shouted.

Miguel halted in his tracks and covered my mouth with his hand. I thought about licking it.

"This doesn't concern you," a voice I recognized as Ted, Miguel's vampire friend, responded. "Keep walking."

"I don't believe we'll be doing that," a third man said. "What's going on here?"

We peeked around the corner, and sure enough, there was Ted with one of the unconscious half-souls over his shoulder, another at his feet, and four unfamiliar half-soul males surrounding him. One approached Ted, and from the way he was walking on a slant, I suspected he'd been hitting the bottle. Plus, his fists were clenched and he looked madder than an old wet hen. Seemed like the human was hankering for a fight.

"Listen very carefully, wolf," Miguel whispered in my ear, still covering my mouth with his hand. "I'm going to step over there to deal with the humans. You're going to wait until they're focused on me, and then you're going to quietly, but quickly, head in the other direction. And you will not stop until you are out of town and back with your pack. Have I made myself clear?"

I tried to think of a way to stay with him. I might help by...help by... Yeah, no way to end that thought with anything helpful I could do. I was doing much better than earlier that day, true enough. But just because my veins no longer felt like they were going to burst didn't mean I was anywhere near as strong as Miguel or Ted. Plus, Ted wanted to kill me, so getting involved meant I'd be trying to help him at the same time I'd be trying to avoid him. That was a surefire way to distract Miguel in the midst of a battle. I sighed in frustration.

"Ethan." Miguel said my name for the first time. He didn't call me wolf. I supposed that meant he was serious. "Do you hear what I'm saying to you?"

I nodded and he dropped his hand. Miguel took two steps forward, then paused, turned on his heel, and returned to me. He gazed into my eyes for several long seconds, and then he dipped his face and kissed my cheek.

"I won't forget you, Ethan Abbatt," he said. And then he really did walk away.

Seconds later, I heard the start of a scream, then a gurgling sound. I peered over to where the half-souls had gathered and saw the one who had been walking toward Ted down on the ground with his hands around his neck, trying to stem the flow of blood. Miguel was standing above him, red dripping from his claws.

"I believe my friend told you to keep walking," he growled at the other half-souls. "This is your last chance to listen to his advice. Because if you don't walk away now, you won't be walking. Ever."

Lord, he sounded cold and cruel. I did as I'd been told and walked in the opposite direction, quickly but quietly. It sounded like at least one of the half-souls hadn't taken

Miguel's generous offer, because another scream rent the air. This one was cut off just as quickly as the first, so I reckoned the half-soul had been injured, or worse.

Okay, so I might have underestimated how dangerous Miguel was. Maybe I even underestimated how dangerous it was for me to be in Kfarkattan. But I was right about what was important: Miguel was my true mate. That meant my home was with him. Even if he was a vampire and a male and, all right, I'll admit it, a bit of a ruffian.

Because if I knew anything, it was to be grateful for whatever blessings were sent my way. Nature hadn't gifted me with much in my life, and I was starting to suspect that my share of the good stuff had been set aside because I'd been slated for a whopper: I had myself a true mate. Now I just had to figure out how to prove it to him.

CHAPTER 5

YOU want to know the good parts about me leaving Miguel and going back to my parents' den? First, my parents were fast asleep, so they didn't know I'd left pack lands, which meant they hadn't been fretting. End of list.

Were you waiting for something else? 'Cause I can't give you no more. That was the only pro. Truly.

I know you might be thinking another good part was that I hadn't been injured in the fight with the half-souls, but here's the thing—it wasn't as if I was fit as a fiddle anyhow. The paralyzing feelings inside me weren't new: lungs that seemed unable to open enough to take in necessary air, heart pushing so hard I swore it was fixin' to beat out of my chest, skin so tight it almost burned. Those kinds of pains were the reasons I'd never been able to keep up with the other cubs in the pack. So, yeah, the discomfort, the pain, they weren't new.

What *was* new, though, was that I finally felt like I knew how to remedy it. For the second day in a row, I'd not only stopped hurting, but I'd shifted. And both things happened after I'd been wounded.

I was quiet as a mouse when I got home, tiptoeing

into my bedroom and then slowly shutting the door so I could lift it a tad and prevent the hinges from squeaking. I shucked off my shirt and pushed my shorts down, leaving them where they dropped on the floor. Then I knelt in front of my dresser and gently wiggled the bottom drawer open. I kept all my extra whatnots in that drawer, so I had to dig past worn paperbacks, a pinecone that struck my fancy a couple of seasons prior, a photo album, three pencils, a smooth rock, and an eraser shaped into a tree silhouette by repeated and strategic use, and then I found it. My pocketknife.

Wearing only my drawers and clutching the knife tightly, I walked over to my bed and sat on the brightly colored quilt my mother had spent hours stitching. I didn't move. Heck, I was barely breathing. I just held on to that knife and considered my next step.

My hand trembled as I pulled out the blade and set it against my wrist. It seemed backward, I realized, hurting myself to stop the pain. But it had worked before. I pressed down and watched the skin turn red, then white, and then, just as I was about to pierce through, I pulled the blade back.

This wasn't a decision I should make in the middle of the night after a long, emotional day. I forced myself to peel my fingers off the knife and set it on my nightstand. I'd get some sleep and figure out what to do in the morning.

"Who is Miguel?" my father asked when I walked into the kitchen the following morning.

I froze.

"You was calling his name in your sleep, Ethan," my mother added softly. She wiped her hands on a towel and set it next to the sink before walking over to me. "Is he one of the vampires who attacked you and your friends?"

I understood why that was her first thought. After all, she knew everyone I knew. I rarely left pack lands without my parents, and when I did, it was with their permission and other pack members were always there.

"It sounded like you was crying." My mother hugged me and petted my hair. "You're safe now. They can't hurt you none here."

My night hadn't been peaceful. That much was true enough. I had tossed and turned, dreaming of Miguel, aching for him. By the time I woke, I was sweaty, frustrated, and more exhausted than I'd been before I went to sleep.

He was one of the vampires from the other night, obviously, so that was true too. And he had injured the others, true again. But the kind of attack he'd waged on me wasn't anything my mother could imagine. I trembled at the memory of his scent, his taste, his hands on me. Lord, I needed him.

My father, misreading my reaction and concerned about my lack of verbal response, pushed back his chair and stood. "We know you must be right petrified about what happened, but your mother's right. The bloodsuckers won't dare come onto pack lands. That there Miguel will never be able to get to you here."

Hollow, that was how I felt upon hearing those words. My eyes were wet and I was practically gasping for air. My father was right. Vampires and shifters didn't mix. The feud between our kinds was so long-standing, so assumed, that I honestly had no clue how it had started. It just was.

My mother squeezed me tightly. "Ethan, son, you'll be fine."

"How about we shift into our wolves and go for a run?" my father suggested. "I ain't ever had a chance to run with you."

No, he hadn't. I had often longed to run through the woods with the other males, hunting and enjoying nature in all her glory. And I knew my father was disappointed that he'd not had that experience with his only son. On the tail of the comments about Miguel, my gut said my days on pack lands were numbered, which meant my father might not have that opportunity again. He was due. We both were.

"Okay, Pop. I just need to, uh, do something right quick. I'll meet you outside shortly."

He nodded and I walked into my bedroom and shut the door. I already knew what would happen if I tried to shift, but I decided to give it a go anyhow. After removing my clothing with shaky hands, I opened the window, crouched on the floor, and called my wolf.

The pain was blinding, literally blinding. Everything went black as I tried with all my might to shift into my other form. My heart felt like it was going to explode, I couldn't breathe, and then I felt a warm trickle on my upper lip. It drizzled down and I darted my tongue out to get a taste. Blood.

I knew what to do. Letting my wolf rest, I breathed deeply and tried to calm my body. When I could see again, I swiped the back of my hand across my nose, wiped away the blood, and stood on weak legs. My pocketknife was still on the nightstand. I took it with me as I climbed out the window.

Hiding behind one of the trees next to the house, I opened the knife again. I was still nervous, but also determined. My father deserved to run with his son, and I wanted this memory to take with me, whether to the grave or to wherever it was I'd have to go to be with my mate for as many days as I had left. So this time, when the blade pressed down, I didn't stop.

Not when I felt the sharp pain. Not when I felt the hot flow of blood drip down my skin and onto the ground. Not after the first cut, nor the second. Not even when I lost count of how many slashes covered my arms and legs. I didn't stop until my hands turned into paws so I could no longer grasp the knife.

Taking in a deep breath, I reveled in the ability of my lungs to fully expand. A few moments alone was all I allowed myself before I trotted over to the front door and yipped.

My mother popped her head out a minute later. She laid her hand on her chest and gave me a watery-eyed smile. "I do declare, son, you are a gorgeous wolf. We didn't see you walk out here so we reckoned you was taking your sweet time. I'll let your father know you're ready to run."

The screen door slammed shut and I heard my mother call out, "Gerald, you might should get a move on. Ethan's waitin' on you."

It was better than I ever imagined. Running with my father, I mean. He was a kind man, and while I knew he loved me, in human form he wasn't particularly affectionate. He was different as a wolf, though. Nudging me with his snout. Jumping on me playfully, his front paws on my back as he barked quietly and then darted away, asking me to give chase. We ran for hours, hunted rabbits, and then napped in the shade of the trees before running again. It was a special time, one I knew I'd hold close to my heart always, and I was grateful to have been able to hang onto my wolf the entire time.

As the sun sank on the horizon and the sky darkened, I could feel the blood I'd lost regenerating. Well, that wasn't it, exactly. I could feel my heart working harder, my lungs faltering as I tried to take in deep breaths, my veins throbbing. Now that I knew what to expect, I reckoned that meant the effect of that morning's bloodletting was wearing out.

"There y'all are," my mother said when we got home. "Go on and get washed up. I have supper ready." She was smiling and drying her hands on a towel. Her hair was slipping out of her ever-present bun, and her long, flowered dress was belted with a white apron embellished with eyelet around the edges. The whole picture was so familiar, so comforting, and I knew my days of experiencing it were numbered. A heap of emotion flooded me. I shifted back into my human form, rushed over to my mama, and threw my arms around her, then buried my face in her neck.

"I'm glad you had a nice day with your father," she whispered to me. Then she patted my back and cleared her throat. "All right now, no more lollygagging. I done made pork chops, and they're gettin' cold."

I lay awake in bed that night and waited until I was certain my parents were fast asleep. My sheets smelled like sunshine and pine 'cause my mother hung them on a clothesline in a clearing surrounded by trees. The scent of vinegar was there too—she used it to mop the floors.

A tiny wooden box sat on my nightstand. It was a construction project I'd made with my father when I was barely starting school. My sister had painted it. That was one of my earliest memories: Crissy sitting on the floor, a cup of water on one side, a few paints on the other, and a faraway look in her eyes. That look became familiar over the years. It was the same one I'd seen the day prior.

I flipped on the light and picked up the box, examining Crissy's art for the first time in years. A full silver moon graced the top of the picture, beams shining from it. The golden sun was barely peeking up from the bottom edge. And between the two, there was a person alongside a wolf, running toward the sun.

I'd always reckoned the drawing was of me and my sister. She had painted it, after all. But now that I looked more closely, I realized the person didn't have curves, the shoulders were broad, and the long hair was black, not my sister's dirty-blonde color. I shivered.

All right, then, time to move on along. I had me a mate to track.

I climbed out of bed and found a piece of paper and a pencil. It took only a few seconds to jot a note down for my sister. It was the only one I'd write. I'd leave it in Crissy's mail slot and she'd explain things to our parents, to our pack. She'd know the right words.

The big question on my plate was whether I should go after Miguel in man form or as a wolf. I'd be able to make better time in my wolf form. But even if I could shift, which wasn't a sure thing, I didn't think I'd be able to maintain the shift. Plus, I'd have nothing to wear when I returned to my human form.

With the decision made, I put on my shoes, stuffed a couple of changes of clothes, all the money I had, and the wooden box into a knapsack, then grabbed a jacket. I folded Crissy's note and slipped it into my back pocket, planning to deliver it on my way off pack lands. Then I opened the window and climbed out.

A quick stop next to the tree where I'd shifted earlier was first on my agenda. I rescued my pocketknife from the ground, spit on it a few times, and then wiped it on my pants leg until it looked clean. I folded the blade inside and dropped the knife in my pocket as I took a long look at the only home I'd ever known. I wondered when and if I'd return. Tears welled in my eyes, but I blinked them away.

No crying. It was time for me to fish or cut bait, and I wasn't going to be sad about it. I was twenty years old. A man. For the past couple of years, I hadn't been sure I'd live this long. I hadn't been sure I even wanted to.

Now I'd been rewarded for my patience and my pain: I had a true mate, and I could shift. If both of those things had come in unexpected ways, well, they could join the club with the rest of my existence. Nothing worth having comes easy, that was what Crissy done told me. She had a solid track record for being right about most all things, so I reckoned this weren't any different. I had a chance at a life here, for however long it lasted. And I wasn't fixin' to give it up. Not for anything or anyone.

CHAPTER 6

I'D spent the entirety of my life in Miancarem, so you'd have thought finding one vampire in the neighboring town wouldn't have caused me grief. Well, you'd have been wrong.

Miancarem proper was all tree-filled hills and mountains, and I knew every square inch with my eyes closed. Kfarkattan, the closest town, the one where Miguel lived, was a two-hour walk away. It wasn't big enough to call a city and I'd been there several times with my folks, so I should have had my bearings. But the thing was, we only ever went into town to buy supplies, and even then we barely chatted to the half-souls, never interacted with them other than to exchange money for goods. So I had no connections, no idea where anything was save for a couple of shops. Well, a couple of shops and the bar where we'd found Miguel and his coven that first night, but I'd already sought him out there and had come up empty-handed.

By the time the night was drawing to a close, I'd looked all over hell and half of Georgia and hadn't found my vampire. Heck, I hadn't caught whiff of *any* vampire. Not knowing where else to search or what else to do, I was fixin' to call a close to my hunt for the night. I figured I'd hole up somewhere, get some rest, and then try again when the sun went down.

But then I heard a sound. Come to think of it, "heard" might not be the correct description, because it was so faint, it was more a feeling than a sound, really. Whatever it was, I heard it, felt it—a steady drumming, a comforting beat—and I followed it without thought.

Down a curving cobblestone street, past darkened buildings, through an alley, and then I was in a particularly run-down part of town, in a musky corner, staring up at a nearly windowless building. I'd seen these structures a time or two from afar and heard tell they were used by them half-souls for storing goods.

The thumping rhythm I'd followed was inside, but it was changing, getting faster, more desperate. I recognized the thought to be peculiar as soon as I had it—how could a noise be desperate? But it was.

I'd never been accused of bravery, and in that moment, I'd have given half of Texas if for once that wasn't so, if just for once I could be someone different, someone stronger. But I couldn't. I could only be me.

So as I approached the eerie building, I was shaking like a leaf, my heart beating so fast and strong, I swore it was fixin' to pound itself right out of my chest. It was such a loud noise, in fact, that for a moment I thought it had drowned out the other sound, the other beat, but then I realized what I was hearing was a combination of the two thumping rhythms. They had joined together, and though everything seemed too fast, too panicked, there was also a hypnotic comfort in the duet.

I wound around the side of the building and found a door ajar.

"You have to stop, Miguel! Please, listen to me. Get ahold of yourself before it's too late."

I recognized the voice right away. It was that vampire, Ted. The one who had helped take the humans home. The one who had wanted to kill me. I pressed my back to the wall and tiptoed toward the voice.

"It's already too late, Ted! He's consumed with bloodlust, feral. Did you see the number of humans he drank tonight? I've never seen anything like it. Not in four decades walking the earth. Nobody needs that much blood. Nobody. And he wouldn't stop. You saw it yourself."

That voice was familiar too. It was Ralph, the vampire who done pinned me to the wall that first night. The one who'd been fixin' to kill me. Huh. Seemed like a universal characteristic among them vampires. Well, all but one vampire, anyhow. Ralph was still talking.

"He wouldn't stop. We have to put him down before he draws us any more attention. As it is, the humans are starting to notice the spike in fights and injuries, the loss of memory after a night out. It's only a matter of time before they stop dismissing it as hangovers and illnesses. And then they'll realize everything coincided with our arrival and they'll be suspicious. We can't let him take away our opportunity to populate the new city."

I had no idea what he meant, but it didn't matter. Nothing mattered. Because at that precise moment I heard a sound that tore me up from the inside out. It was a shriek, a growl, and a cry all mixed into one. And it was made by Miguel. My mate was hurt. I quickened my pace and came to the edge of a wide open space.

Half a dozen vampires were huddled together at one end of the room. They were looking at the crumbling brick wall in front of them. Or rather, they were looking at Miguel, who was attached to that wall.

Heavy metal chains were wrapped around both his wrists and ankles, along with his neck and belly. His gorgeous hair was damp and tangled, hanging in front of his face. His clothes were filthy and ragged. And he was yanking at the bindings, trying to break free, making noises that sounded more animal than man.

One of the vampires I didn't recognize jumped into the conversation. "I hate to say it, but Ralph is right. Tonight isn't the first time he's lost control. We all know he's always had a voracious appetite, but it's gotten worse since we came to this town. And the past few days..." He shook his head and shuddered, letting the thought trail off. "Miguel needs to be stopped. We have no choice. He has to be put down."

"Fine, he needs to stop," Ted agreed. "But killing him isn't the way. Besides, how do you propose to do it? He's stronger than any of us, stronger than anyone I've met. Miguel Rodriguez isn't easy to kill. You might have been able to combine forces and catch him off guard while he was feeding, but make no mistake, you will not be able to get close enough to take off his head or stab his heart. Not without putting yourself in grave danger."

Miguel was screaming, his chains clanging, as the vampires argued with each other.

"There has to be a way," Ralph insisted.

I twisted around the corner, and Miguel froze, tilting his nose up and darting his face all about. The sudden quiet seemed to perplex the other bloodsuckers. They stilled and stared at their captive. Fear poured off them, which was peculiar as all get out, considering they were free and he was restrained.

"What's going on?" one of the vampires asked. "Why is he being quiet all of a sudden? Why did he stop moving?" They began talking all at once, trying to agree on a plan, urging each other forward to kill him. All except Ted, who looked more sad than scared. Or maybe it was regretful.

I was rooted in place, not sure what to do, not sure how to help. Then, just as fast as it had started, the silence was gone, replaced by what I could only describe as a roar. Miguel struggled against the chains, more riled up than he'd been prior, moving so fast it was difficult for me to track what he was doing.

The voices got louder as the vampires realized they were in a heap of trouble. Suddenly, Miguel got one arm free. They were eat up with fear by then, turning on each other, shoving whoever was near toward the threat while trying to back away.

But it was too late. After his first hand was free, Miguel kicked his foot loose and yanked the rest of the chains off like they were made of string. Then all hell broke loose.

Miguel stood in place, gasping for air, a few links still hanging off one ankle, as he glared through the strands of his hair. Surprisingly, he wasn't staring at the vampires in front of him, the ones who had been planning his demise but were now screaming and tripping over themselves and each other trying to escape right quick. No. Somehow, even though I was shadowed in darkness and almost completely hidden by the wall, Miguel must have known I was there. Because the distance wasn't stopping him from landing his piercing gaze straight on me.

Somebody with any sort of sense would have turned and run for the hills. I wasn't that somebody. Instead of fleeing from danger, I stepped forward, leaving my makeshift hiding spot and revealing myself to a room full of vampires. I was as nervous as a rooster in a henhouse, but I hoped it didn't show. Or at least not much.

"Blood," Miguel growled.

"You see?" Ralph shouted. "Even now he wants to feed. It's bloodlust like I to—"

"Look," one of the other vampires said, interrupting him. He'd been watching Miguel, had followed my mate's line of sight as he made his way toward me, so he was the first to realize I had entered the room. "Who is that?"

The vampires moved aside, giving Miguel a wide berth as he stalked me. The chain still attached to his ankle dragged on the ground, making a loud scraping sound. He huffed out loud breaths, his chest heaving. The other vampires whimpered and gasped, terrified he'd come after them.

They needn't have worried. My mate had eyes only for me. But not in the way you'd think. Or at least not how I would've thought. Not that I'd ever had cause to consider how my mate would look at me, mostly because I'd never reckoned I'd have me one. Anyhow, if I would have imagined how a reunion between mates would go, it wouldn't have been all ominous sounds, fearful cries, and glaring killers.

So, yeah, the situation was lacking in the romance department. Also, there was a real upsetting degree of homicidal overtones. But by now, it should be clear how I chose to deal with those problems—I put one foot in front of the other and walked toward my destiny. Whether I was slated for imminent death or a great love was anybody's guess at that point. I reckoned either option was a real possibility. Didn't matter none. I refused to run from my mate, come what may.

"That's... Is that...?" Ralph squinted at me as he stammered. "It's that shifter." He turned his gaze to the other vampires. "That's him, right? The one from the other night?"

"Blood," Miguel growled again. "Your blood. I smell it. Why?"

He seemed to be doing better, if the length of his sentences was any indication. Not that he was writing sonnets or anything, but he'd moved past grunting.

"Shit!" Ted said. "Miguel scented his blood and now

he's going to feed from him."

I heard several gasps.

"He can't," one of the vampires said.

"They're poison," another added. "Feeding from a shifter is a death sentence."

Ted took a step toward us, though it seemed fruitless at that point because Miguel had near about reached me and everybody else was too far away to stop him. And from what I'd just overheard, distance wasn't the only thing that would prevent Ted, or the other vampires, from getting in Miguel's way. He was stronger than the rest—the strongest. I was right when I'd pegged him as Alpha.

"Ted, don't get in his way," Ralph said. "This is perfect."

"Perfect?" Ted asked, his tone making clear he figured Ralph was more than a couple sandwiches short of a picnic.

"Yes. You asked how we could stop him. You said he was too strong for any of us to get close enough to deliver the deathblow. Well, we don't have to do a thing. Miguel's bloodlust is going to take care of the problem for us."

"No." Ted sounded stricken. "We can't let him do that. It's a horrible way to go."

"There's nothing we can do," a vampire said.

"At least it's fast," another added.

After that, I tuned them out because Miguel was within arm's reach. I had been walking toward him, but stopped, letting him take the final steps, bracing myself for whatever was to come. I heard shuffling, noticed movement in my peripheral vision as the vampires skedaddled toward an exit lickety-split, and then there was silence. Well, other than Miguel's heavy breathing. And the dragging chain. And our pounding hearts. But other than that, silence.

My mate didn't stop until he was inches from me. I looked up and met his gaze, felt his breath on my face. It was coming out too quickly. His forehead was creased and his eyebrows scrunched, as if he was in pain.

"Miguel?" I said as I reached a trembling hand out and rested it on his hard chest. "Are you all right?"

"I can smell your blood," he said and wrapped his long fingers around my wrist, flipping my arm so the underside was showing. That was where I'd cut myself that morning, and though the wounds were healing well, certainly faster than they would if I wasn't a shifter, the marks were still clear. But they were no longer bleeding, so he shouldn't have been able to smell my blood.

"I'm fine," I said, instinctively trying to keep my voice soothing. It was only after the words came out that I realized what I was doing. I wasn't scared. Some part of me had already decided that Miguel didn't pose a danger, that his question was based on concern for my well-being rather than the bloodlust the other vampires had mentioned.

He traced the fading scars on my arm with one finger and the brown in his eyes bled until it was all I could see. "Who hurt you?" he asked through clenched teeth, his fangs slipping over his lower lip. It should have terrified me, but instead I found it exciting, arousing. I wanted those fangs on my flesh, *in* my flesh.

"Is it true what they said?" I asked. "Is it true that you'll be hurt or...or worse if you feed from me?"

I already knew the answer to the question. Shifter blood was deadly poisonous to vampires. That was a given. But something inside me balked at the idea, refusing to accept it. At least not when it came to this particular vampire.

As I stood in front of Miguel, I could feel my veins thickening, feel more and more blood flood my system. It was like my body was reacting to his presence. First, by sending blood south so I had a raging erection—a peculiar reaction, sure enough, but it felt good. And also by producing more blood in general—peculiar *and* painful. I'd need to release it soon, or my organs would ache and then start shutting down right quick.

"Who hurt you?" he repeated. His nose twitched, and he dipped down, running it against both of my arms, my neck, across my chest, until he was squatting before me, moving his face over my legs. "Here," he said and looked up at me. His face was smack dab in front of my groin. "There's blood here." His hand was on my right thigh, where I'd wiped my knife. I dressed to the right, so his fingers were close to my swollen prick. I moaned. "Who hurt you?" he asked again, his voice louder, angrier. Then he reached down to his foot and yanked on the metal chains, snapping them like they were twigs.

"Nobody," I panted, arousal flooding me. His presence was all it took to get me going. It was incredible and terrifying all at once.

He bowed up, jumped to his feet, and, in one swift motion, he clasped my wrist and lifted it so the marks were right in front of my face. "Don't lie to me, Ethan. I smell your blood. These are new marks." He was fit to be tied. "Who. Hurt. You?"

"I'm not lying, honest. I made those marks. I drew the blood."

"Why?" Miguel sounded genuinely concerned, near about torn up. He wrapped one arm around my waist, drawing me close, and cupped my cheek with his free hand. "Why would you hurt yourself, wolf?" His voice was softer, gentler. Lord, I wanted him.

"I didn't... I wasn't..."

It was nigh on impossible to concentrate with my mate so close, with his hands on me. I wanted to feel his bare skin against mine, wanted to taste his lips, wanted to mate. So much. But before I could have any of those things, I needed to address his concerns. I took a deep breath and let it out slowly, trying to calm my frazzled nerves.

"I didn't want to hurt myself, but I had to let the blood out. There was too much, and I couldn't shift. I could barely breathe," I said, my air coming out in short gasps once again. "Like now."

"You're having trouble breathing?"

He eased closer, as if he was trying to feel the breaths leaving my body, measure them. His mouth, so close to my neck, captured my entire focus. Vampires fed from the jugular. It wasn't the only place, but it struck me as one of the most intimate. I trembled and whimpered with need.

My hand was in my pocket before I could think about what I was doing. I pulled out my pocketknife and took a step back, trying to make my fingers work enough to get the blade open.

"What are you doing?" Miguel asked. He covered my hands with his larger ones. I tried to shake him free. "Stop, wolf. Stop!"

I raised my gaze to meet his and wondered if it looked as frantic as I felt. It was too much. Everything inside me was too much. My heart was working so hard it felt as if I was being stabbed in the chest. My lungs had no room to expand. Even my stomach was cramping up.

I licked my lips and opened my mouth, but I couldn't get my tongue to work. "Hurts," I finally managed to gasp out.

It didn't seem like enough of an explanation, but Miguel somehow understood. He kept his gaze locked on mine as he lifted my arms until my wrists were in front of his face, then he dipped forward and pressed his lips to my pulse point. "I can hear it," he said. "It's so loud." Then he looked down at my skin and his gaze flicked back to mine, his eyes wide. "Your veins," he gasped. "They're huge. Are they always—"

My wail interrupted his sentence. My knees buckled and the pocketknife clattered against the floor. It was the end, I was sure, and though it was coming earlier than I had hoped, at least I'd get to die in my mate's arms, for which I was thankful beyond measure. I rested against his hard body and closed my eyes.

"Ethan?"

I heard the concern in his voice, but there was nothing I could say to comfort him, nothing I could do. As the blackness enfolded me, I had only one thought: *Mate.*

CHAPTER 7

THE sharp fangs piercing my skin were the only thing that kept me from falling under. How I recognized it for what it was, I couldn't rightly say. I mean, I'd never been bitten by a vampire. And it wasn't as if I was operating on all cylinders.

Whatever the reason, I knew right quick that Miguel was biting me, and as much as I'd wanted that very thing, I couldn't let him do it, couldn't let him sacrifice himself for me. Particularly because it was a hopeless cause. If I didn't die that day, I'd die soon after. The affliction that had plagued me all my life was at its worst, and I knew there was no way for me to survive it. But I refused to take my mate down with me.

"No," I managed to say as I tried to wiggle away from him. "Poison."

He tightened his grip on one arm and held my head in place, but at least he pulled his mouth back. "Stay still, wolf," he demanded.

I wanted to refuse, wanted to stop him, but I wasn't strong enough to put up much of a fight when I was at my healthiest. At my weakest, I didn't stand a chance.

"There's too much blood. I'll spit it out, but we need to

release it."

He leaned forward, his fangs once again touching my skin. I'd seen him bite some of my pack mates and pull back right away, preventing much blood from getting into his mouth and spitting out the rest. That hadn't damaged him, so I expected this wouldn't either. With that thought in mind, I ceased struggling.

Though I'd tried to stop him, there was no denying how much I craved what was coming. I stretched my neck and went loose in his arms, giving him complete dominion over me. This time, when his fangs sank into my skin, I moaned and arched up, trying to get closer instead of pulling away.

It didn't hurt, which surprised me. Even more unexpected was the overwhelming arousal that washed through me when Miguel started drawing the blood out of my veins with strong, long sucks.

"Oh!" I cried out. "That's... Oh, oh, oh!"

There were no words to describe what I was feeling. My body was hot and shivery all at once. Every square inch of skin felt hypersensitive. And the exquisite release as my blood was pulled from my body was akin to having every single vein stroked.

I clutched his shoulders, digging my fingers in, holding him close as I moaned and cried and begged him not to stop, never to stop. And when one of his hands made its way into my pants, my shouts of joy ricocheted off the walls in the huge room as I pulsed over and over, coating his palm and my drawers with more seed than I would've thought possible.

When my hips finally stopped thrusting, my seed no longer spilling, I grappled with his pants and released his erection. Hard, so hard. The skin was smooth, and his member fit perfectly in my palm. I moved my hand over him as if I'd been doing it all my life, as if giving him pleasure was the most familiar thing I knew. I squeezed his testicles, rubbed my thumb over his crown, and made my way up and down his pole, trying to give him the same joy I'd just experienced.

All the while, Miguel continued stroking me, inside and out, with his hand in my pants and his fangs in my throat. He had kept me hard, kept me wanting, and when I heard his muffled groans and felt slick pre-ejaculate seep from the head of his erection, I knew I'd shoot right along with him.

It could have been seconds or it could have been minutes. There was no way for me to know because time stood still, and all I felt, all I heard, all I smelled was my mate. I was consumed by a sense of all-encompassing rightness. As if, finally, finally, my body was doing what it was meant to do.

Somewhere along the way, we crumpled to the floor. But we didn't stop touching, and Miguel didn't stop feeding, until both of us were limp and sated, coated in semen and shaking with pleasure. Miguel pulled his fangs back and lapped at my skin, immediately stemming the flow of blood.

"How?" I asked.

He kissed over the spot he'd been licking and then along the underside of my jaw up to my lips. "Our saliva closes the wounds."

"Mmmm," I sighed contentedly as I lay in Miguel's

arms, luxuriating in postcoital bliss, feeling relaxed and easy in my skin, my body lax and lethargic. Lord, I felt good. He felt good. I couldn't keep the grin off my face as my eyes drifted shut.

And that was when it hit me—Miguel had fed from me. And not just a small amount. I gasped as I shot up to a sitting position.

"What is it?" he asked, rising fast as lightning and wrapping his body around mine as he darted his gaze around the room, searching for whatever threat had startled me.

"You...you..." I raised a trembling hand to his face and felt his cheek, his lips, his chin. "You said you weren't going to drink me." I swallowed down my rising tears, and my voice broke as I finished speaking. "I don't want to lose you."

Panic overwhelmed me, my body shaking like a leaf. And then I felt two large hands cup my face, and warm, soothing breaths ghosted over my lips. "Shhhh, wolf. I know what I said, but your blood is different. It tastes as good as it smells. Not like sulfur and rotting fruit, like other shifters."

Hearing that I tasted different from my kind didn't surprise me. I'd been different all my life. But neither did it alleviate my concern about his well-being.

"But what if it can still hurt you? Even if my blood doesn't smell the same or taste the same as other shifters, what if—"

"No." Miguel was adamant. "You're not poisonous. I've walked the earth long enough to know what to avoid. My senses are very well developed, wolf. Besides, with as much as I fed from you, I would be gone already if your blood could harm me. And, as you can see, I'm perfectly fine." He paused and crinkled his forehead, looking thoughtful. "Actually, I'm better than fine. I'm not hungry." He swallowed hard. "I'm always hungry, always. Even more so lately. But now"—his wide-eyed gaze met mine—"I'm not." He was quiet for a few beats before he spoke again, his voice hushed. "What are you?"

"I'm, uh..." I didn't know how to answer his question. I wasn't even sure what he meant. "I'm a shifter," I finally said. "You know that, already."

He nodded. "I've seen you in both forms, seen you shift. But your scent... I can sense that you're a shifter, and yet... You don't smell like the others, don't taste like the others, and your blood"—he trembled—"there's so much. And it feels different, warmer, heavier. It feels—"

"Right," I said. "It feels right." I blushed when I realized I'd interrupted him. He stayed quiet, watching me with those deep, knowing eyes, waiting for me to continue. So I did. "My blood in you, I mean. It feels like it's supposed to be there, like you were meant to feed from me." I paused when I realized he hadn't responded at all. "That's what you were trying to say, isn't it?" I whispered.

He nodded slowly, his gaze never leaving mine. "That's exactly how I feel. How can you know that?"

"Because I feel the same way," I answered hoarsely.

"The same way?" He repeated my words, the question clear from his inflection. "How do you mean? Does it have to do with what you called me?"

I lowered my gaze and chewed on my bottom lip nervously. "Well, maybe not exactly the same. I mean, I don't feed on blood, but—" The second part of his question registered and I tore my gaze up and stared at him. "What I called you?"

"Yes, before I fed from you. Your heartbeat was sluggish, your veins ready to burst, I thought you were going to pass out, and then you called me 'mate.' I wasn't certain at first, but then you said it again when you came." He shuddered and dipped his face, nibbling at the sensitive skin behind my ear. "You're so beautiful, wolf. Your brown hair streaked with auburn and gold, those smoky eyes, and full lips. Stunning. And when you're in the throes of pleasure... Going on four hundred years and I've never seen anything like it." He closed his eyes and I felt his breaths come out faster. "I don't know what's happening to me. I've never—"

I ran my fingers through his soft hair, and his words halted as his eyes flew open, landing on me, lust and awe shining out. He moaned and scooped me closer, then took my face in his hands and tilted it before pressing his lips to mine in a kiss that started molten and somehow managed to heat up from there.

His hands were everywhere at once, tugging my shirt up and over my head, yanking my shoes off my feet and pulling my pants and drawers down right after. And all the while, he kissed me, held me, nibbled on sensitive skin. By the time he had me curled in his lap, bare other than my socks, I was erect once more.

I wouldn't have thought it possible. Never before had my body given me pleasure. I hadn't had trouble behaving because even in the privacy of my own bedroom, taking myself in hand hadn't been appealing, but now, with him touching me, pleasure was all there was. I was amazed by how he made me feel.

"And just how is that, Ethan?" he asked. It took a spell before I understood what he was asking, partly because I hadn't intended on speaking out loud, and also because my mind was awash in a haze of arousal. "How do I make you feel?" he repeated as he traced a prominent vein in my swollen prick with one long finger.

"Alive," I replied on a gasp. I clung to his shoulders and thrust my hips up, seeking his touch, needing it.

He cupped the back of my head and lowered me onto my back as he chuckled. "I make you feel *alive*, do I? That's ironic."

"Huh?"

The smile he graced on me was tender and sweet. He traced my lower lip with his thumb before bending over me and skating his mouth over mine. "I need to taste you," he said. "With as good as you smell, as delicious as your blood tastes"—he bored his gaze into me—"I can't resist you, wolf."

He'd already fed from me, and I had no concern about him doing it again. But when his kisses dipped lower than my neck, I realized I hadn't understood what he meant to do. He lapped at my clavicle, and I trembled, surprised the light touch could evoke such strong feelings. When he covered my nipple with his lips and swirled his tongue around it before suckling it, I keened and tangled my fingers in his hair, holding him in place.

Miguel didn't deny me. He kept on his task, working the pink nub until it was swollen and sore. Even then, he wasn't through with me. He simply moved from right to left and drew the other bud into his mouth in just the same way. I gasped and moaned, writhing beneath him and grasping any part of him I could—shoulders, hair, arms. And then, just when I was certain another climax was upon me, Miguel circled his hand around the base of my shaft and squeezed tightly, halting the crest.

"Damn, you're thick," he said as he stroked me from base to tip, "and long." I shook, the need he created overwhelming me. "Can't wait to taste you."

And then he did something I hadn't expected. He moved his head down and drew my erection into his hot, wet mouth, swallowing down my rod like he had my blood.

"Miguel!" I cried. "Mate!"

I couldn't have stopped the tidal wave from crashing had I wanted to. And I wanted nothing of the sort. I gasped and moaned as I spent myself in his mouth and he swallowed down every drop of my offering. I couldn't raise my head, couldn't move my limbs. My chest heaved as I panted, trying to take in more air. And all the while Miguel stayed where he was, petting my hip and licking at my crown. Eventually he twitched and shouted as his hot cream splashed on my leg.

"I was right," he said, looking up at me, his lips swollen and eyes heavy-lidded. "You're delicious."

I reached for him, feeling like I was going to fly right apart without his weight to keep me grounded and safe. He took my hand in his and kissed my palm before crawling over me until his face once again hovered above mine.

I took a deep breath, gathering every ounce of strength I possessed. "How much do you know about shifters?" I asked.

Miguel Rodriguez was my mate, which meant I was going to stick to his side like white on rice. I reckoned it was only fair for me to explain that to him.

"I know that none of them have ever felt as good as you."

I frowned and a growl rumbled out at the thought of my mate feeling anyone, ever.

Miguel smirked. "That's adorable," he said, dipping down and tugging my lower lip between both of his before nibbling his way across my jaw to my ear. "I know quite a bit about shifters, actually. For example, I know your kind are very territorial, and based on that noise you just made, I'm guessing you're trying to stake a claim on me."

Oh, there was no "trying" about it. "You're mine," I nearly shouted. "And you best realize it right soon."

The grin left his face, and he looked truly regretful when he cupped my cheek and responded. "I'm not a good bet, wolf. I tried to warn you before, tried to tell you to stay away."

"That's never going to happen," I said adamantly. "I belong with you, and that's all there is."

"I'm a vampire," he said, as if that explained anything.

"You're my mate," I replied, knowing that trumped everything. "My true mate."

"Vampires don't mate, Ethan. We don't settle down and build dens and raise puppies. We're not monogamous. We—"

"Oh, well, you surely are now," I told him. "There's going to be nobody but me for you from here on out."

"And how do you plan to explain me to your pack?" He sounded frustrated. "Like I said, I know all about shifters. I know your kind looks down at everyone different. Humans are lesser beings, half-souls; that's what you call them, right? They can't shift into two forms so they're not worthy. And bloodsuckers," he scoffed. "We're worse, aren't we? Dirty, soulless, immoral."

"I never said that," I said hurriedly, feeling sickened by his hostile tone and harsh language.

"No, you didn't. But do you deny that it's true? Shifters live in packs, live *for* the pack, and you're never going to bring me home to meet your mother. So how, exactly, do you plan on this going?"

He was right, of course, and it wounded me deeply, the fact that he'd never be accepted by my pack, the fact that I'd have to leave them in order to live by his side.

"I don't deny it," I whispered sadly. "But I hope that my mama will come into town to meet you." I wiped the back of my hand across my eyes. "Either way, I'm staying with you. That's where I belong. That's where my loyalty lies now."

"You'd choose me over your pack?" he asked skeptically. "You'd leave pack lands to live with me?"

It was the only choice I could make, the only choice I wanted to make. Like I'd said, Miguel was mine.

"Yes," I answered simply, because, well, it was just as simple as that.

CHAPTER 8

"You barely know me," he said.

"I'll get to know you better over time," I countered.

He tried again. "I'm not a good man."

"Well, if that's true, I'll teach you how to change. Because you can rest assured that I surely *am* a good man."

Whatever other faults I had, and there were plenty, my mama'd always told me that my heart was pure. I had to believe it would be pure enough to cleanse my mate of whatever sins he believed made him unworthy of our mating.

"This isn't a game." His voice was getting louder.

"Who said I was playing?" I lowered my volume.

"You're not hearing me, wolf," he said.

"I hear you loud and clear, *vampire*." I grinned when his eyebrows shot up. "But fate is fate. You're mine just as much as I'm yours. Surely you feel it."

He shook his head and furrowed his brow. "I don't feel a thing."

I didn't pay his words or ornery expression any mind. He had to feel the bond. It was unmistakable, absolute. And I was fixin' to say so when we heard muffled voices.

"We're about to have some company." Miguel

scrambled for my clothes and shoved them at me. "You need to get dressed and get lost."

I dropped the shirt he'd just handed me and folded my arms across my chest. "Try again," I said, standing tall and proud in my naked glory. It was quite a feat, seeing as how I was neither tall nor, at that exact moment, firm. Though I was pretty sure a few more minutes with my mate could rectify that problem.

His jaw dropped and he gaped at me. "How is it that you don't fear me?"

I thought about his question. I'd come upon him right after he'd fed from humans until they lay unconscious at his feet. I'd seen him nearly eviscerate my pack mates. Even the other vampires were scared of him. But to me, he'd been caring and tender, and when push came to shove, that was what I considered important.

"You've never given me cause to fear you, Miguel."

His eyes softened and he kissed my forehead. "I'm glad you feel that way, wolf, but you should be afraid. Just being here is dangerous. The men you saw earlier? The ones who tied me up? They're coming back."

"You can recognize their voices from this distance?" I asked, amazed by his strength.

"You heard them too," he pointed out.

And I realized he was right. We heard the vampires at the same moment. I just hadn't spent enough time with them to be able to identify them, but maybe if I knew them as well as Miguel...

"Ethan, I need you to take your clothes and leave. They're not stable, they're in a group, and if something happens to you..." He shook his head, his expression pained. "Please," he said. "I need to know you're safe. I realize that doesn't make sense, but I just—"

But it made perfect sense. I was his mate, and though he was trying to deny it, he could feel the bond, same as me. He didn't want to see me hurt. And the man wondered why I didn't fear him? I grinned inwardly.

"Where's your den?" I asked him.

He was shaking out my clothes, but paused in reaction to my question. "I don't... What?"

"Your den."

My shirt was pulled on over my head. "I'm a vampire," he said as he dressed me. "We don't have dens." My underwear and pants were next. "We've been over this."

"Well, all right, then, what do you call your house?"

"My..." He shook his head. "Listen, we don't have time to keep talking about this." He shoved my shoes onto my feet and then stood, pulling me up with him. "You need to go."

"That's what I'm rightly trying to do," I said. "I'd be havin' an easier time of it if you would tell me where you live."

"Why?" he asked, his tone making his exasperation clear. The hands flying up clued me in too.

"Because the sun's coming up soon."

"Meaning?"

"Meaning that's where you're going to be during

daylight, and I'm fixin' to stay by your side."

He shook his head and dragged his fingers through his hair. "Wolf, you need to leave. Go home."

"I am home."

"I already told you that I'm nobody's home!" he said forcefully through gritted teeth.

I didn't bother responding, I just looked straight at him and didn't flinch when he growled and paced back and forth in front of me. The voices had been getting louder, and I knew the vampires would be walking in any minute. Apparently, Miguel came to the same conclusion, because he grabbed my bicep and pulled me toward the end of the room, close to where I'd entered, rescuing my knapsack from where I'd dropped it on the way. Without releasing me, he pulled a key out of his pocket, unlocked a door, and flung it open.

"There." He pointed to a set of stairs leading down into the dark. "That's where I'm staying. It isn't clean, it isn't romantic, and it isn't permanent." He gave me a pointed look, and I knew he was talking about more than his living space. "But we're out of time, so for now, it's the safest place for you."

He released me and slipped the strap of my knapsack over my shoulder. I took a step down.

"Ethan," he said, his voice softer.

I turned around.

"Can you recognize my scent from a distance?"

I'd never been able to scent as well as other shifters, but then again, I'd never been able to release my wolf. Since

I'd started shifting, I'd noticed a change, an improvement. But even without my wolf senses, I had no doubt I'd know Miguel.

"You know I can," I said.

"Good." He nodded. "If you scent or hear anyone, and I mean *anyone*, other than me coming down these stairs, you move the bookcase wedged in a corner and use the escape tunnel."

"Where will the tunnel take me?" I asked.

"Where will..." He sighed in frustration. "It'll take you away from danger, away from here."

Away from him. That was what he meant. Well, I wouldn't use the tunnel, but I saw no sense in arguing with him about it. He'd be able to concentrate on whatever needed doing with the other vampires if he felt like he'd won that go-round with me. So I nodded and slowly moved down the stairs, surprised at how well I could see in the dark. As soon as I heard the door close and lock, I tiptoed back up and sat smack dab in front of it, waiting for whatever would come next.

TURNED out a solid wood door didn't do a thing to prevent me from hearing every word spoken on the other side of it. While I was glad to be able to monitor the happenings in the next room, I knew I'd need to keep still and quiet if I didn't want to be discovered. Though it shouldn't have been an amazing feat, I'll tell you I was relieved as can be that my body cooperated with me on that count.

I was still getting accustomed to it, my seemingly new body. No more pangs and cramps that made me twitch and groan. No more tightness in my chest that had me gasping for air and feeling light-headed. No more aches in my limbs and swelling in my veins. My insides felt like they finally matched my outsides, like I fit.

What Miguel had done to me wasn't something I could match with a pocketknife. No wounds, no pain, and so much blessed release. I shivered with the memory of him drawing out my blood and caressing my skin.

"Miguel?" Ralph's voice was a fair bit shaky and a whole lot surprised.

"In the flesh," Miguel answered darkly.

"How'd you... I didn't mean to..." Ralph was sputtering, more nervous than a long-tailed cat in a room full of rocking chairs.

"Oh, damn, I was so worried." That was Ted. I heard footsteps quicken and figured he was racing toward Miguel. "Are you okay?" He paused. "You look better." Another pause. "You look really good, actually."

"I feel good," Miguel answered. Though he didn't raise his voice, he somehow managed to sound scary as could be when he said it. "No thanks to any of you."

Ted didn't reply, but the other vampires were doing the verbal equivalent of tripping over themselves to apologize and make excuses.

The sound of a whimper quickly followed by flesh hitting flesh brought every other noise to a halt. Miguel's grunts didn't sound pained, so I knew he wasn't being hurt. That knowledge kept me behind the door. And though I'd sworn to myself that I'd stay still, I couldn't hold back a wince when I heard vampires begging and crying. By the time the violent sounds finally stopped, I was equal parts sick and grateful.

"Have I made myself clear?" Miguel asked, and I wondered whether I'd missed part of the conversation because he hadn't said anything in some time.

Several voices responded with a breathless "yes" and though I recognized them as being the same vampires who had restrained Miguel, none of them were Ted or Ralph.

"What's that, Ralph?" Miguel said.

There was no reply, and I wondered why Ralph wasn't answering. Lord, if I had to hear any more begging and crying I was sure I'd retch.

"I can't hear you." Miguel's tone gave me goose bumps. If it had been directed at me, I might would have soiled myself.

"Miguel," Ted said nervously.

"You going to tie me up again, Ralph?"

"Miguel." Ted was firmer.

"Because you need to understand that if you do it again, you'll be done." He paused. "I'm not hearing an apology. Maybe I should just go ahead and finish you off now. Don't put off until tomorrow what you can do today. Isn't that how the saying goes?"

"Miguel!"

"Stay out of it, Ted," Miguel snapped. "This doesn't concern you."

"Damn it, Miguel! You know full well that he can't talk because you're crushing his windpipe."

"Oh, am I?" His tone dripped with sarcasm. "Oops."

"He made a mistake and he knows it, just..." Ted paused. "Please, give him another chance."

After a moment I heard gasping and coughing. What I didn't hear was an apology.

"What happened with the shifter?" Ted asked, sounding anxious. I wondered whether he was trying to change the topic and take Miguel's attention away from Ralph. If so, it worked.

"He isn't your concern." Miguel's tone held a note of warning.

"This was the third time he showed up in as many days," Ted said. "I just want to make sure he's been dealt with so we don't have any more surprises."

"I took care of him," Miguel said.

"If any wolves go sniffing around looking for him, they won't come close to here, right?" Ralph asked. His voice was raspy and weak, but I recognized it. "Where'd you dispose of the body?"

He barely got the last word out before I heard an "oomph" sound followed by coughing and whimpering.

"Okay," Ted said. "I think Miguel made his point. The

sun's coming up soon. I'm turning in." I heard footsteps and mumbled words, and then Ted spoke again. "Miguel?"

"Yeah," my mate answered.

"Do you need my help with, uh—" He paused. "With anything?"

"Yeah, you can keep fucking Ralph the hell away from me. I shouldn't have let him walk out of here. He messes with me again, and no matter how much you ask, I won't give him another chance."

"I know. Thank you. He just...he was worried. We were all worried. You always feed so much, and until this town grows, we need to be careful."

"I know that!" Miguel said. "I'm older than you, Ted. I don't need a school lesson on blending in."

"Well, you haven't been blending," Ted answered in a voice so low it was almost a whisper. "If anything, you've been feeding more than usual since we got here, not less. You can understand why Ralph thought you'd gone feral."

"I was hungry."

Ted snorted. "You fed enough to fill three vampires for months. That was just today. And you said you were still hungry." He was quiet for a beat before continuing. "You had me scared, Miguel. I thought we'd lost you."

"I wasn't feral," Miguel sighed. "I was hungry."

"You don't look hungry."

"Do I look feral?" Miguel retorted.

"No," Ted answered.

"Good. Then it's settled. I'm turning in."

I heard Miguel's footsteps coming toward me. I recognized his gait by sound alone.

"Let me know if you want some company," Ted said, his suggestive tone making my hair stand on end.

I couldn't hold back my growl. I clenched my hands into fists at my sides and my entire body stiffened, fixin' to pounce out of the room and eliminate the threat to what was mine. A key turning in the lock tore me out of my jealous haze. I stepped down one stair to leave room on the landing for Miguel.

He opened the door just wide enough to slide into the room, and then closed and locked it behind him. I opened my mouth to say something about Ted's offer, but Miguel's lips over mine stopped any words from coming out. He tangled his fingers in my hair, and I whimpered into his mouth, melting against him, submitting completely.

We were both breathless when he finally pulled back. He held his pointer finger in front of his mouth and shook his head, telling me without words that I needed to keep quiet. The space was large and there was nothing filling it, so any noise we made ricocheted off the walls, echoing loudly. We started walking down the stairs and hadn't taken but a few steps when Miguel scooped me up in his arms and held me tight against his chest.

I gasped in surprise, and he gave me a self-satisfied smirk, curling up one side of his lips, his gaze pure sin. That expression should have been frightening, but instead it made me hard, made me squirm. With a knowing gaze, Miguel lowered his eyes to my groin and licked his lips. Then he started moving across the room, his feet not making a sound.

Faster than I would have thought possible, we were at the end of the room. Miguel opened another door and took us through it. Then he squatted down and set me on a soft mattress, kissing my forehead before standing back up. I put my knapsack down and squinted, my gaze following him as he closed and locked the door and then lit a candle.

Oh, Lord. Miguel in candlelight. My stomach dropped.

"So," he said, smoothly pulling his shirt out of his jeans, "when I told you to come down here, you took that to mean that you should sit at the top of the stairs and eavesdrop?"

Whether he was expecting me to answer, I couldn't rightly say, but it wasn't going to happen. Not when he was slowly pushing each button on his shirt through the buttonhole, exposing smooth, brown skin and rippling muscles. I reckoned the fact that I was able to keep my tongue in my mouth and drool off my chin was an accomplishment.

"Did you hear everything, wolf?" he asked. When I didn't respond, he paused in his task and raised one eyebrow.

I needed him to keep going, so I swallowed thickly and nodded. He kept working on his shirt but his heated gaze didn't leave mine.

"I hurt those men up there," he said. "A lot."

I didn't say anything, but neither did I turn away from him.

"And Ted's offer to keep me company?" His shirt now draped completely open, he started working on his jeans.

"He was talking about a very specific type of company."

My lips curled up, exposing my teeth, and I grumbled deep in my chest.

"It wouldn't have been the first time I'd kept that kind of company with him." I saw a flash of regret in his eyes as he spoke, but he kept right on going. "The same is true for other men. Other women. You need to understand—"

Before he could say another word, I shot off the bed and slammed him against the wall. He gasped in surprise, and I took advantage of the distraction, cupping the back of his head and pulling him down so our mouths could connect. My need for him was frantic, all-consuming, and I knew his was the same because instantly we were kissing, thrusting and twirling our tongues, grasping at skin, pulling on hair. And when we had to move apart, just to take in air, I licked at his jaw, his cheek, his neck, anywhere I could reach, maintaining every connection possible between us as I shoved his clothes out of the way and began working on my own.

"You're mine," I said into his mouth as I nibbled on his lips. "Just mine."

"You don't understand," he said, but he didn't stop kissing me, lapping his tongue at mine. "I can't—"

But I did understand. And I needed to make sure my mule-headed mate finally got it. We'd managed to get his clothes off completely in all our grappling, and the sight of him in the flesh nearly took my breath away. He was so beautiful. Powerfully built. Mouthwatering. And he was mine.

I panted and moaned and clasped his arms tightly,

maneuvering him toward the mattress. He was bigger, stronger, so he could have stopped me if he'd wanted to, but he didn't, so within seconds, I had him prone in front of me. I shrugged out of my shirt, shoved my pants and drawers down, and stepped out of my shoes. Then I lay on top of my mate and tugged on his ear with my teeth.

"Can you feel that, Miguel?" I asked him.

He pushed his bare backside up and ground it against my erection. "It's pretty hard to miss, wolf. Like I said before, you've got *some* dick."

I blushed, but didn't let the raw language stop me. "Not that," I whispered into his ear. "I'm talking about what you can feel in here." I reached my hand underneath his body and rested my palm over his heart. "You're my true mate. That means our souls are connected. Right here."

He shook his head, pressing his face into the sheet. "Vampires don't have souls. Isn't that what your *pack* teaches?"

For less than a second, I hesitated. I'd always heard exactly that. But... "No," I said. "That's wrong. I can feel the bond. Our souls are connected. Mine and yours. That means you have a soul."

I would have thought a vampire wouldn't pay no mind to what shifters thought, but he relaxed beneath me, and he sighed softly, telling me different. My chest was flat on his back, my legs draped on top of his, one hand against his heart, the other at his side, and my chin was tucked over his shoulder, my mouth right by his ear.

"Miguel?" I whispered as I rubbed his bare skin.

He grunted.

"I reckon there're lots of things I done learned that don't hold water, and I'll hear you if you care to set me straight. But when I tell you that you're my home, when I say you're my true mate, that there ain't no storytelling."

Again, he didn't respond with words, just stayed quiet beneath me. But he moved one hand to my hip and rubbed circles on my skin.

"You keep on talking about other people—that Ted, them other males and females. I suppose you're trying to scare me off. But there's no other for me except you, and I aim to keep you to myself, hear? I know I'm smaller and younger, but if I have to die fighting off your other admirers or earning my place by your side..." I sighed, knowing that was exactly what would happen, knowing I could never measure up to all the worldly people Miguel knew, knowing I could never best vampires in a fight. "Well, then, I reckon you'll know what it meant to have a shifter for a mate. A true mate."

CHAPTER 9

"ETHAN?" Miguel said quietly.

I was lying on him, inhaling his scent, kissing the smooth skin behind his ear, loving that he was letting me.

"Yeah?"

"I'm warmer," he said as he covered my hand with his and pushed it firmly against his chest. "Can you feel that? We're usually cold. Vampires. Right after we feed, our temperature rises slightly. But it's never been like this." He shuddered. "It feels good. I feel good."

"I feel good too," I said. "Healthy." I licked at his neck. He tasted so fine.

"You shouldn't." He looked back at me over his shoulder and frowned. "With how much I fed from you—" He shook his head. "That was more than I should have been able to take from half a dozen men without weakening them." He flipped over, and suddenly, I was on my back with my mate pinning me to the bed as he looked into my eyes. "I never would've hurt you, wolf. I didn't lose control. But you had so much blood. More than any other, human or shifter. Did you know that?" His voice caught and his nostrils flared. "I could hear it, feel it, pulsing strong and hot."

I licked my lips and then chewed on the side of the lower one, my gaze not moving away from his.

"The first time I ever shifted was that night we met," I said. "Your, uh, friend had clawed me, remember? He had me pinned to the wall, and I'd lost so much blood, and—"

Miguel wrapped his arms under my shoulders and pulled me up against him, holding me tight, so tight. I didn't want him to stop, loving the feel of his body pressed against mine, reveling in the idea that he wanted me. But when I found myself gasping for air, he loosened his grip, apparently realizing my predicament.

"I'm sorry," he said sheepishly. "I don't know what came over me." He closed his eyes, took in a calming breath, and then looked at me. "Please, continue. You were saying that you only recently started shifting. But I thought shifters took their wolf forms from a very young age."

"We surely do," I said. "The males. All but me, I mean. I never could. But, yes, male shifters take their wolf form young and lose their hold on their human side as they get older, so they need to tie with a female to secure it. Female shifters have a strong connection with their human side, so strong that they can't shift until they accept a tie from a male."

He scoffed. "Damn, your kind is superstitious. So many rules to keep everybody in line."

I furrowed my brow. "What do you mean?"

"Never mind." He shook his head. "Go on. You were saying that males shift young but you couldn't. Why?"

"I've been sickly all my life, so we reckoned that was the cause." I shrugged. "We figured I wasn't strong enough to take my wolf form."

He ran his intelligent eyes over my face, and then he dipped down and sniffed my neck. "You look good, wolf. Healthy. I can't scent any illness in you."

"That's the funny thing about it," I responded, chewing on my lower lip again. "Like I said, I do feel healthy. Now."

"Now?"

"Yes. What you did to me earlier..." His gaze turned carnal, and my cheeks heated yet again. "Not that," I clarified. "I mean when you fed from me." I trembled and my voice turned husky. "It was so good, like you were drawing out the weight and the pressure, like you were making everything fit. I don't hurt no more."

He furrowed his brow, contemplating what I'd said. "So you were able to shift for the first time when Ralph injured you. And you cut yourself, made yourself bleed because you hurt so much. And now, after I fed enough to drain another man, now you feel healthy?"

I nodded.

"That's strange," he finally said. "I know a healer who can come take a look at you, try to figure out what's going on."

"I reckon I know already."

"You do?" he asked, sounding surprised. "What is it?"

"You're supposed to feed from me," I answered.

"I'm supposed to feed from you?" he repeated,

enunciating each word slowly.

I nodded. "It makes sense, right?"

"How does the idea that a vampire is *supposed* to feed from a shifter make sense? Your kind is poisonous to mine."

"But I'm not poisonous to you, right? I mean, that's what you said. You fed from me and you feel good now, better than before you fed from me. So you see? You feel better. I feel better."

Miguel peered at me again, giving me that piercing stare of his. I got the sense nothing passed his notice, and I wondered whether his wisdom came from his age or if he'd been this way before he was turned.

"And you're thinking this is all because of that mates thing," he said. "Am I right?"

"True mates," I answered firmly. "We're true mates."

"What exactly does that mean?"

"I told you already," I said. "True mates are connected deep inside, at the heart, at the soul. We're two halves of a whole. That's why we have to tie with each other. Nobody else will do."

With as often as Miguel gave me that wicked grin, it was amazing that it still made me squirm, but I gasped and wriggled under him when he did it again.

"Is this all an elaborate story concocted to get me to turn over for you, wolf? Because you need to work on the contradictions. Besides, it isn't necessary." He reached between us and circled his big hand around my pecker. "I'd love to feel this thick dick deep in my ass."

I moaned and thrust up into his hand. "That's not... I didn't.... What contradictions?"

"You said male shifters have to tie with female shifters, right?" he asked. "That whole business about females being connected to their humanity and males being connected to their wolf. But then you said true mates can tie only with each other."

He was stroking me in slow, even pulls, his hand warm and right and perfect. It was hard to concentrate. "Yes," I said. "That's right."

"If I'm your true mate, Ethan," he whispered into my ear, his hot breath making me tremble, "that means you can't tie with anybody else."

"Can't," I said. "Won't. Promise."

"Well, then, how're you going to hold onto your human half, wolf?" He rubbed his thumb over my crown, spreading the early seed that had formed there. "I'm not a female shifter."

I tangled my fingers in his hair and pushed his head up so I could look into his eyes. "I told you already, I ain't never been right. In my human side, I hurt. My wolf couldn't come out. But when you fed from me, everything got better."

"Yeah, I got it. You have too much blood in your body, and it kept your wolf down. But what does that have to do with your true mate tying rule?" he asked.

He was too big, too strong for me to flip him over, but I managed to get out from under him and climb onto his back, tucking my chin over his shoulder and speaking directly into his ear.

"We tied together in the way of your kind, vampire," I said. "You pierced me with your fangs, drew out my blood." I trembled with the memory of how good that had felt, him feeding from me. "Your tie healed me, released my wolf. And you said it helped you too, said you feel better, warmer." I rubbed my erection against his backside. "Will you let me tie with you in the way of my kind? I know you don't need it to take a wolf form. I can't rightly say that I need it to hold my human, but"—my voice shook with desire—"will you let me inside, Miguel? I want you."

He stretched out and started moving off the mattress, so I thought he was denying me. But then he fumbled on the floor and reached back, thrusting something in my direction. I picked up what he held in his palm and squinted in the low light, trying to make out the words.

"It's cream," Miguel said. "With what you're packing, too much will be barely enough." I had no idea what he meant, so I stayed as I was, perched on his back looking at a container of hand cream. Miguel looked over his shoulder and met my gaze. "I know you're new to this, wolf, so take my word for it."

Then he turned back around and wiggled until he was settled comfortably on his belly, resting his head across his folded arms. It was awe-inducing, having such a strong, large man lying before me, putting himself at my mercy, in my care.

I knelt above him, straddling his hips. With my free hand, I caressed his skin reverently. It was cooler than mine, but not cold, definitely warmer now than he'd been when we'd necked in the street. I scooted down as I touched, running my hand over his broad shoulders, his muscular back, his rounded backside.

When my fingers came close to the crease, he spread his legs and pulled his knees underneath him, holding his body like a frog. That position raised his behind higher and spread his cheeks, leaving what was usually hidden to the world exposed to me. I trembled as I moved my hand into his trench, fingering the hot skin gently, getting closer and closer to the puckered rosebud in the center. When I gave a barely there drag with one finger, he moved and canted his backside even higher.

I kept my finger on that target, rubbing circles around it, wanting to push inside. That was when I remembered the cream I'd been handed, and its purpose became apparent. I fumbled in my initial attempts to open the lid, my hands shaking so hard in anticipation of what was to come that I couldn't get a good grip. Eventually, I managed to pry the lid off the blasted container and coat my finger with the thick, slick substance inside.

"Fuck, yes, Ethan," Miguel moaned when I coated his entrance with the cream. His crass words caused a tightening in my lower region, ramping up my arousal. "Feels good," he added breathlessly. I dropped the cream, whimpering as I rushed to squeeze my erection in order to keep myself from spilling in reaction to his heated tone, to the knowledge that I evoked those feelings in this intimidating, powerful, stunning man.

Brown eyes looked at me over a muscular shoulder. "Are you okay, wolf?" Miguel asked.

I nodded, my head bobbing quickly. "Want you so much," I gasped. "I've never—" I gulped. "Never felt like this." I blushed. "Sorry," I said. "I know I'm inexperienced and—"

"I've never felt like this either," he confessed, his eyes softer, his smile warmer. "C'mere, baby." Miguel gestured with his chin, indicating that he wanted me to lie on top of him once more. I did as he asked, and he reached for the discarded cream, dipped his fingers inside, and scooped out a generous portion. Then he straightened his left arm, supporting all of his weight on it, and reached back with his right, coating my throbbing prick in the cool, slippery substance.

"Miguel!" I shouted and shook, instinctively thrusting forward into his fist.

"Shhh," he whispered and pushed back as he encouraged me to move forward, not stopping until the smooth, rounded head of my penis pressed against his inviting entrance.

He moaned and rocked back, circling his pelvis, then moved his hand to my hip and pulled me forward, and before I knew it, I'd pressed through a tight ring, and I shouted and cried and begged until I was completely connected to my mate, buried in silky, tight heat.

"Oh," I gasped. "Oh, Lord."

"Good?" he asked, his voice rough.

I collapsed on top of Miguel, pressing my chest to his back and circling my hips against his firm globes. I brushed my lips against his nape, tasting his sweat-slick skin. "So good," I whispered.

He stroked my thigh and then raised himself to his hands and knees beneath me. "For me too. Now show me what you can do with that monster, baby."

I wasn't sure I'd be able to do anything but spill my seed, but the need to thrust was undeniable, leaving me unable to stay still. I moved my hips back, shivering at the exquisite pleasure of hot skin dragging across my hard length, and then I shoved forward, gasping along with my mate, the pleasure nearly overwhelming.

Somewhere along the way, my brain shut down and instinct took over. I slid in and out of his channel at a frantic pace, grunting and gasping, and Miguel met every pump, pushing back, begging for more.

"Yeah, baby, like that. Damn, you're huge, stretch me so good. Yes, Ethan. Yes!"

"Ugh," I groaned, mindless with need and desire.

My already impossibly hard rod swelled further, getting thicker, longer, and then, just when I thought I couldn't take another moment of pleasure, I felt my mating knot pushing against Miguel's pucker.

"Holy fuck!" Miguel cried out. "What is...what is..." I shoved forward and circled my hips at the same time, wedging my way inside my mate's body. "Ahhh," Miguel shouted, never slowing his movements. If anything, he pushed back harder against my prick, locking the mating knot within his warm channel.

That desire, that need in my mate was my final undoing. I opened my mouth wide and clamped down on Miguel's shoulder, close to his neck, my sharp canines breaking skin and claiming the vampire as my mate. My body stilled, breath caught, and I pulsed long streams of hot ejaculate into the warm body cradling me. With my last rational thought, I slid a hand around for Miguel's prick and stroked him once, twice, a third time, and then his hot release coated my hand as he cried out my name in bliss.

His arms gave out and he collapsed on the bed with me on top and still inside him. Both of us gasped for air as our hearts raced, keeping the same rapid beat. Miguel managed to move his arm back and patted my leg.

"Damn, baby, you're incredible," he said.

I kissed his back, feeling warmed by the endearment and the praise.

"Yeah?" I asked shyly. "That was okay?"

"No." He shook his head and then looked back at me over his shoulder, his gaze connecting with mine. "It was much better than okay." He clenched his passage around my still buried prick, locked in place by the knot at the end. "So this is what you meant by tying? Much as I know about shifters, I didn't realize your bodies, uh, changed this way during sex."

"Does it bother you?" I lowered my eyes as I asked the question. "It'll pass right soon."

"C'mere," he said, moving his hand to my bottom and nudging me up as he stretched his neck toward me. Our faces met in the middle without our bodies separating. He touched his lips to mine, flicking out his tongue. "When it passes, I'll just want you to do it again," he mumbled against my mouth as he tilted his hips and ground his backside against me. "You feel good inside me, baby. Perfect."

I sighed and settled on top of him, resting my cheek against his back, feeling relaxed and settled. "Miguel?" I said.

His body felt loose beneath mine, his breathing slow and steady. "Yeah?"

"I'm glad it was you," I whispered, not knowing whether he'd understand what I meant. I was glad he was the one I could touch, the only one who'd ever touch me. I was grateful beyond measure that Miguel Rodriguez was my true mate.

He was quiet for several minutes, still and solid beneath me, so I thought he'd fallen asleep. I closed my eyes and felt myself drifting off to dreamland with my mate's body beneath mine, his scent surrounding me. I'd never been more comfortable, more content.

"I'm glad too, Ethan," he whispered quietly. "More than I know how to say."

CHAPTER 10

I'D never had cause to know how vampires spent their days. That they holed up somewhere and stayed out of the sun was a given. But whether they crawled into coffins and died, or played Parcheesi until sunset, I couldn't rightly say. Well, it turned out they didn't do either of those things.

It was daylight outside; at least that was what I reckoned based on the time. But in Miguel's underground den, it was dark and cool. We lay tangled together under a soft blanket, snug as a pair of bugs.

I came to a few times during the night, er, day, and each time I was being held protectively, cradled within Miguel's strong arms, my head tucked under his chin, one of his knees wedged between mine, my testicles and flaccid pecker resting against his thick, muscular thigh. I sighed contentedly and burrowed closer to my mate, ready to fall back to sleep, when he kissed the top of my head and petted my back.

"How're you doing, baby?" he asked. "Any regrets?"

Just hearing him calling me "baby" was enough to make feeling regret nigh on impossible. "Nuh-uh," I said and squeezed him tightly. "I'm keeping you."

He chuckled, causing his chest to vibrate against me.

"Is that right, wolf?" He tangled his fingers in my hair as he spoke, massaging my scalp.

I tipped my head back and met his gaze, wanting him to know that I was serious as sin. "Yes, sir, it surely is."

He didn't argue about it this time, just took in a deep breath and then let it out slowly, rubbing the back of my head and my nape all the while. When he dipped his face and kissed my forehead, my breath caught and I was flooded with a new desire. Well, maybe it wasn't new, maybe I just finally knew it for what it was.

"You're hungry," I said to my mate.

"I'm fine," he whispered against my skin, kissing me again, still petting gently.

"I know, but you want to feed. I can feel it." I tilted my neck and stretched toward his mouth, giving him complete access to my exposed skin.

"No, Ethan. I already drained you more than I should have. Losing too much blood can be dangerous, even for someone with your condition."

"My condition?" I furrowed my brow in confusion.

"Yes. Your body produces too much blood, right? That's what you said. Like I mentioned, I know a healer who'll be able to take a look at you and let us know what's going on and what we can do to help fix it."

"No," I said firmly. "I don't need to see a healer because there's nothing that needs fixin'. I don't produce too much blood."

"But—" He started arguing, but I wasn't having none

of it.

"Before I met you, before I realized I had a true mate, it felt like too much, sure enough. But now"—I grinned at him—"the way I see it, I'm making enough blood to nourish my mate. That there's just the right amount." I beamed at him. "So you see, everything happens for a reason, just like my sister always says."

The way Miguel smiled at me would have melted me into a puddle if I wasn't already there. Vampires were supposed to be cold, heartless, but his twinkling eyes and gentle smile were anything but.

"Damn, are you ever sweet, wolf," Miguel said, his voice full of longing. "Sweet and tempting. But draining you again right now would be dangerous." He sighed regretfully. "Don't worry, I'm fine. I'm used to being a little hungry, that's just how it is for me. Especially lately." He lowered his mouth and kissed the pulsing vein in my neck. Almost immediately, he gasped and pulled back, his eyes wide with surprise as he stared at me. "Can you hear that?" he asked breathlessly.

"Hear what?"

"Your blood." He licked his lips. "It's so loud, rushing through your veins, flowing strong and full. Feels like it's calling to me again." He shook his head and furrowed his brow. "I don't understand it."

"That's because you're not listening to me." I smiled wryly at Miguel as I spoke. He really was as stubborn as a mule. "We're true mates. Two halves of a whole. You say it feels like my blood is calling to you? Well, I say your need called to me and my body is doing what comes natural and responding." I paused and watched his face, making sure he was absorbing my words. "Go on," I said, tilting my neck again. "Take what you need."

"Are you sure?" His voice was rough, his breathing faster, louder. "I don't want to hurt you, baby. Never want to hurt you."

My chest tightened and I blinked my eyes rapidly. "You won't hurt me. I trust you, mate."

Desire burned in his eyes and his nostrils flared, so I figured I'd said something right.

Miguel kissed my neck again, but this time, he opened his mouth and sucked on my tender skin, then licked at it. "You taste so good," he said. "Never tasted anyone like you."

A growl escaped without my permission, the knowledge that my mate had fed from another not sitting right, despite the fact that he'd been walking the earth for several lifetimes.

He pulled back and rubbed his thumb across my lower lip, the grin on his face equal parts amusement and regret. "You are a jealous little thing, aren't you?" he said.

I waited to bristle at being called small, my size having been one of my lifelong sources of shame. But the way he said it sounded fond, not belittling. Besides, I liked how my smaller body seemed to fit so perfectly with Miguel's bulkier frame, like two pieces of a puzzle that clicked just right.

"You weren't complaining about my size last night," I said cheekily. "Or, uh, this morning, I guess," I added, my confusion over night and day ruining the intended haughty effect.

Miguel reached between my legs without a second of hesitation, like he knew he had the right to touch there. He curled his fingers around my testicles and stroked upward, pulling my prick through a tight vise before going back down and starting the process again.

"Ungh!" I moaned and raised my hips, trying to get closer to his touch.

Every inch of my genitals was touched, manipulated, heated.

"You know," Miguel whispered into my ear, his breath ghosting over my neck and causing a full-body shiver. "Blood flows all over. And I can be very creative." He gave my pecker a squeeze before continuing his ministrations. "Do you still want me to feed from you?"

"Only me," I panted, intense desire for the man next to me causing my air to come out in short, fast bursts.

He cupped my cheek with one hand and traced my eyebrows with the fingers of another. "After four hundred years, I didn't think anything could surprise me, but I didn't see you coming, wolf."

I tangled my fingers in his long, silky hair and looked into his eyes. "Can you do that? Can you feed just from me?" I took in a deep breath and let it out slowly before adding, "Can I be enough for you?"

He searched my eyes, hesitating before answering my question. "It's been done," he eventually answered. "Not often. And those who have tried it usually..." His voice trailed off and he swallowed thickly. "But, yes, I can feed from you alone, Ethan."

Miguel didn't bury his fangs in me right away. Instead he rolled me to my back and lay on top of me, nipping at my lower lip, then dragging his lips across my jaw and nibbling on my earlobe. All the while, his hands were just as busy as his mouth, tugging and twisting my nipples, rolling and caressing my testicles, stroking and squeezing my prick. I moaned and writhed beneath him, feeling so right in that position, with a vampire, my *male* vampire, that I couldn't conceive of it being wrong.

"Are you sure about this?" he asked me breathlessly. "Are you sure you want to stay with me? Don't you want to go home?"

"They're one and the same," I answered without hesitation, my voice husky, want and need and something else—something deeper, stronger—coursing through me.

"Okay," he said. "All right." He cupped the sides of my head, petted my scalp with his fingers, and caressed my face with his thumbs. "And, Ethan? I didn't expect you. I don't understand what's happening to me, what's happening between us. But as long as you want to stay with me, you'll be all I need. You are enough for me. Don't ever doubt that, okay, baby?"

I trembled as I nodded and clung to him, digging my fingers into his shoulders. He was talking about more than just feeding, I knew. Then again, I'd been asking about more than just feeding.

"Just a little bit now," he whispered into my ear, still running gentle circles over my head with his fingers. "I'll get you good and relaxed and then you can sleep some more."

It wasn't a question, which was a good thing because I was too overrun with unfamiliar feelings and emotions to answer. My heart felt full to the point of overflowing, but not in the painful way to which I'd become accustomed. This was like a warmth that glowed and beamed from the inside out.

And though he'd fed from me only once, I already missed that pulling sensation of my blood being drawn out, like a caress underneath my skin, and the glorious release that came with it. I arched toward Miguel, whimpering and begging without words, feeling empty without his mouth on me, his fangs in me.

The sharp teeth on my neck were an expected, welcome relief. I sighed and felt the tension leave my body with every drop of blood Miguel took. He pulled back shortly after he'd started, lapping at my skin to quickly close his marks. I whined in protest, blinking my eyes open in confusion. But before I could formulate words, Miguel nipped the sensitive skin above my areola with his sharp fang.

"Ah!" I cried out in surprise, lifting my chest, legs bucking.

Without removing his mouth, he ran his tongue around the perimeter, and then sucked my nipple into his mouth with a deep, hard pull.

"Oh, oh, oh!" I stuttered, panting furiously, grasping my

mate's hair and humping my hips up, trying to find friction.

Miguel clasped my wrists and pinned my arms to the bed. He pushed his thigh between my knees and ground it up against my testicles, the pressure on the edge of too much but somehow feeling just right. And all the while, he continued suckling at my chest, eventually swiping his tongue over my right nipple to stem the flow, before moving on to my left, biting and then suckling and feeding.

Both nipples were red and swollen by the time he released them and kissed his way down my belly. He lifted my legs onto his broad shoulders and looked up at me, his face hovering just above my erection, his gaze wicked.

"Are you ready for one last bite, wolf?"

Anticipation was tinged with a hint of fear as I thought about how to answer. Surely it would hurt to be bitten *there*. I looked down at Miguel, settled between my legs, his gaze glued to mine as he licked my pole, leaving a swath of glistening, slick skin. A corner of his mouth turned up in a barely there grin, and then he sucked each of my testicles into his mouth. Where before he'd been rough and demanding, his passion a palpable thing, now he was gentle, making love to me with his mouth.

"Yes," I said, trusting him implicitly, willing to give him whatever he wanted and trusting he'd make it good for me.

After another few seconds of sucking and licking, he released my testicles and blew a trail of cool air along the length of my rod.

"You're so damn thick," he said as he traced a prominent

vein with one finger. "All this blood pooling together, making you swell, making you hard."

"For you," I said, my voice coming out rough with need.

His eyes burned as he stared at me and took hold of my erection. His red lips opened and curled back and then he dipped his face, just barely piercing my vein before swallowing my prick down to the root.

"Miguel!" I shouted, bucking up reflexively.

It didn't last long; it couldn't. Not with my mate's wet, welcoming mouth taking me in, giving me tight friction as he sucked my hard length and swallowed the hot blood flowing from my vein. He took me higher and higher, relentlessly pleasuring my rod with his mouth as he rolled and fondled my testicles. When I finally came, crying his name and shaking, he sucked harder, swallowing my seed down with my blood as he moaned in pleasure.

My eyes were closed, chest heaving, when Miguel finally released me from his mouth and crawled up my body, peppering me with kisses. He wrapped his arms around me and curled me into his side, tucking my face under his chin and securing one leg around my thighs. I was held tight, protected, wanted.

"Sleep," he ordered.

So I did.

CHAPTER 11

WAKING up alone in Miguel's bed was unexpected and disconcerting. I wasn't used to being in new places, wasn't used to being on my own, wasn't used to being in the dark, literally, about where things were, who was around, what time it was. I took in a deep breath and sat up, squaring my shoulders.

My mate was a busy man. He seemed to be the leader of his pack or coven or whatever the bloodsuckers, er, vampires called their groups. And, if what I'd witnessed the day prior was any indication, it wasn't an easy group to lead. Seemed as if they'd just as soon kill Miguel as follow him.

This was my new life and I best get accustomed to it. I was in Miguel's den, which made it my den now, and if I wanted to know where things were, well, I had excellent night vision. I'd just have to give myself a tour.

The room I was in was tiny, with space for the mattress on the floor, but not much else. And while it wasn't dirty, it was worn, with crumbling walls, a cracked floor, and what I imagined would look like all-around dinginess if there had been a light to turn on, which there wasn't.

Wanting to see the rest of the basement, I dressed

quickly. I took my money out of my knapsack and stuffed it into my pocket. I opened the door and slowly stepped out of the small, dim room and into a larger one. Though the size of the space differed from where we'd slept, nothing else did. There wasn't any furniture, save for a table and a couple chairs near the stairs. And it was just as dreary.

Was this how vampires lived? It didn't match up to what I'd heard about them. They were flashy, self-absorbed, cared only about whatever fun they could have in the here and now. Well, the space I was standing in wasn't flashy or fancy or fun. I'd have to ask my Miguel about that. And while I was at it, I'd ask him whether his kind lived at all.

Though I'd listened to pack members speak about vampires many times, I'd never thought to ask for details about them. Even if I had asked, I wasn't at all sure I'd have received accurate information. Seeing as how I was going to be spending a whole lot of time with Miguel's people from here on out, I reckoned I should know more than vague references and ill-informed rumors.

My growling stomach disrupted my explorations. I was feeling healthier than usual, stronger, but all the activity with Miguel had taken a toll. Though I was loath to admit it to him for fear of making him pull back, having him feed from me was wearing me out. The issue wasn't a shortage of blood— my body produced enough for the both of us. But I hadn't eaten since dinnertime the day prior, and then I'd been up all night and expended energy with Miguel in passionate bursts during the day. Bottom line was that I needed to refuel if I wanted to keep sustaining both of us, and really, even if I wanted to sustain only myself.

Running into the other vampires wasn't something I wanted to risk. My interactions with them up to that point could be summed up as violent and near-death. Seeing as how I wanted to avoid both of those things, I made sure to stay very quiet as I walked across the room. When I passed by the table, I noticed large pages spread across it. I'd never seen paper that size, so it caught my attention. When I looked closer, squinting to make out the small markings, I realized they were huge maps of Kfarkattan and the surrounding areas, including Miancarem, our pack lands. It struck me as odd, particularly because the maps stood in stark contrast to the rest of the nothingness in the space. I made a mental note to ask Miguel about that too.

But first, I needed to find some food. I tiptoed up the stairs, every step slow and deliberate. When I finally made it to the top, I cupped my hand around my ear and pressed it to the door. There was no noise, not even the sound of breathing. I took a moment to process that thought. When had I started being able to hear breathing?

My senses had never been as developed as other shifters, and though things had improved once I'd shifted a few days earlier, having hearing sensitive enough to pick up breathing was beyond even my father's capabilities. And yet, I suddenly realized I'd been able to do just that since Miguel had started feeding from me. For that matter, being able to see at night, with the light of the moon illuminating the woods, was common. But being able to see in pitch dark, with no light source? Not so much. I turned around and peered down the stairs. How was it that I could see anything without any windows or lights in the room?

A growl from deep in my belly, followed by a sharp pang, called my attention back to the task at hand. Food. I needed to get some food. I flipped the lock and then turned the knob slowly, opened the door just a smidge, and pressed one eye to the crack. Nobody was out there.

Once I finally made it out of the basement, I was on the street outside the warehouse in what felt like seconds. Knowing I could be faced with unhappy vampires at any moment, I didn't lollygag, just got out of there as fast as I could while being mindful of the need to keep perfectly silent.

The night air was cool and crisp, bathing my lungs and leaving me feeling fresh. With my hands stuffed in my pockets, I stayed close to the buildings and walked toward Main Street, where most of the shops were housed. Dismissing the crowded diner in favor of the general store, I pushed open the door, causing the bell hanging from it to jingle.

The human at the counter looked up and gave me a careful smile. "What can I do for you, young man?" he asked.

"Oh, uh," I stammered. Though I'd been in the human shops a few times, I'd never been on my own, never had cause to explain myself to anybody. "I just need to pick up a few things, uh, food."

I dipped my head and shuffled away, then walked through the store briskly, picking out a loaf of bread, some fruit, a bit of fresh meat, and a container of peanut butter. That should hold me for a day or two.

"Is that it for you?" the shopkeeper asked.

I nodded and counted out my money without looking up and meeting his eyes. The man was acting right nice, but I was still nervous, not knowing how to behave around a half-soul after spending my life being told to avoid them. 'Course, I'd been taught to avoid vampires too, and we know how well that had turned out.

With the bag holding my purchases in hand, I walked out of the shop and back onto the unfamiliar street. A lifetime living close to this town, closer than any other, and yet it was a foreign place, inhabited by humans I didn't know. Every shifter I knew lived within walking distance, and the urge to go to them, to be with my pack, was strong. But not stronger than the driving need to be with my mate.

I clenched the bag handle more tightly than necessary and trudged back toward the dark, lonely street where Miguel lived. With my jacket collar up, my shoulders hunched, and my gaze aimed at the ground, I had a sense of being almost invisible, like maybe the humans wouldn't notice me among them. And it worked fine. Nobody got close or spoke to me, right up until I was turning off Main Street.

"Ethan!"

I jerked, snapping my head up. Miguel was moving toward me at a fast clip, his lips pressed into tight lines, a pinched expression on his face.

"What's wrong?" I asked, expediting my pace, wanting

to reach him as fast as possible.

Just as soon as we were within arm's distance, he pulled me to him, engulfing me in a hug. "Are you okay?" he asked, pressing his face against my hair.

"I'm fine," I assured him. "What happened?"

He inhaled deeply. If he were a shifter, I would have thought he was trying to take in my scent. When the tension drained from his body and he sighed contentedly, I reckoned that was precisely what he'd been doing.

"You weren't there," he said. "When I came back to the room, you were gone."

I immediately felt remorseful for having worried my mate. "I'm sorry," I said, hoping he could hear the sincerity in my voice. "I reckoned you'd be busy with your...coven?" I paused and pulled back to look at him. He shrugged and then gave me a short nod. Taking that as confirmation that I'd used the correct terminology, I continued. "And I was hungry, so—"

"There's food waiting for you," he said. "I went just as soon as the sun set. I wanted to have it there when you woke up, but I was delayed dealing with Ted and those other guys." He looked me over, his gaze flicking all around my face and body. "And then, by the time I got back, you were gone."

He sounded just as dismayed the second time he reminded me of my absence as he had the first.

"I wasn't leaving you," I assured him.

"I know that," he answered too quickly.

His tone was curt and his gaze dropped to the ground.

Everything about the way he responded told me that I was, in fact, correct in my suspicion. I grinned to myself. Though he'd tried to push me away, it was clear that Miguel didn't want me to leave. He wanted me by his side, hopefully as much as I wanted to be there.

Miguel took the bag from my hand and wrapped his arm around my shoulder, keeping me close. "Let's go," he said and started leading us down the street. "Next time you need something, let me know and I'll take care of it. It isn't safe for you to be out here at night. There are all sorts of dangers lurking around."

"But you said you went out to get me food and you're here now," I pointed out.

The grin I got from the man was devilish. "That's because I'm the biggest danger of all."

My pecker thickened and lengthened in response to my mate's words and tone. Was that weird? I mean, should a reminder of his violent nature be arousing? Before I could give it more thought, we turned the corner and I was lifted off my feet and pressed up against the side of a building.

"Miguel?" I asked, my voice cracking. He wedged his leg between mine and released his hold on my upper body just enough to make my groin drop onto his thigh, pressing my testicles down against the hard muscle. "Ugh," I moaned, a pang of desire shooting through me.

He moved one hand to my neck, wrapping around it until his thumb rested on the front of my throat. I gulped and met his searing gaze.

"I didn't like finding you missing," he said, his voice rough. He moved his thumb in tiny increments back and forth across the throbbing vein in my neck. "Why is that?" he asked quietly, almost as if he was talking to himself. He moved his leg up and around, rubbing my groin with a magnificent friction. "I've been alone for a long time, even before I was turned. Why, all of a sudden, did I feel like something was missing just because you weren't in my bed?"

"Mate," I answered as I panted for air, that one word explaining everything.

He paused, no longer surprised by my response, I supposed.

"And you want this, right?" he said eventually. "You want to be with me?"

I nodded, the motion barely perceptible because of the hold he had on my neck. I was so unbelievably turned on by his strength, his power. By him.

"I want that too," he said. "Heaven help me, but I want you to stay with me. But, Ethan, I will let you go if you say the word. I will never harm you." He paused, looking deeply into my eyes. "You don't need to run away from me. Just say the word and I'll return you safely to your pack."

"I wasn't running away," I croaked, not because of the pressure from his hand around my throat—that was welcome—but instead from the emotion and need that almost overwhelmed me. "I promise."

Miguel dipped his face and pressed his lips against mine. "Okay," he mumbled against my mouth and then nibbled on my lower lip. "I'm glad," he whispered as he mouthed his way across my jaw to my ear. "But if you change your mind, wolf, it's an open-ended offer. I'll get you where you want to be safely, even—" His voice cracked, and I could feel his heart racing. "Even if it isn't with me."

It wouldn't happen, I knew. I'd never want to leave my mate. Separating from a true mate was a death sentence for a shifter. Normally, that was because true mates could tie only with each other, so if a male left his true mate, he'd be unable to tie and, eventually, he'd lose his human form and live out his days trapped in his wolf form searching for his other half.

I didn't see that happening to me. After all, my wolf hadn't been able to come out until I released most of my blood, so having that form take over struck me as nigh on impossible. Before I'd met Miguel, I'd been prepared for an imminent death, and had felt sure I didn't have the strength to keep going. Learning that I generated too much blood to allow my body to take my wolf form was comforting because it gave me a reason. But knowing the issue and resolving it were two different things. Without Miguel there to release the pressure, to draw out my blood, my only option would be self-induced bloodletting. Given how painful and tiring that had been, I doubted it was something I'd be able to keep up for long.

So, like I'd heard about other true mates, I needed Miguel to keep both my forms, to help me stay strong and energetic. But more than that, I *wanted* him. I liked the way Miguel looked at me as if I was something special. I was drawn to his power and strength. I enjoyed his company. And, Lord, was I ever attracted to him.

That attraction was in the forefront of my mind with my mate so close, his breath ghosting over my face as he nibbled on my ears. I rocked my hips, rubbing my groin against his leg, enjoying the friction and the pressure.

"Do you need to come, wolf?" he asked.

I'd never known I could need release as frequently as I had since I'd met him. It wasn't just my blood; my balls hung heavy with seed, aching. I whimpered.

Miguel grinned and nibbled at my lip. "I'll take care of you," he said.

And then I was on my feet, leaning against the wall, and he had squatted in front of me, unzipped my shorts and taken my erection into his mouth. It took almost no time for him to have me shaking and crying out his name as I pulsed long streams of ejaculate onto his tongue.

"Do you know," Miguel asked as he licked the head of my prick, "that your seed tastes as good as your blood?"

He looked up at me and our gazes locked. It was oddly arousing, looking down at a large, powerful man who was on his knees for me. He flattened his tongue and swiped it from the crown to the root and then sucked one ball and then the other into his mouth. He covered my softening erection with his large hand and rubbed it gently.

"I bet I can make you go again." He squeezed my prick and nipped at the sensitive area beneath my testicles, making me yelp and then moan. I felt myself thickening in his hand.

"Yeah," he said, sounding very satisfied with himself and looking smug as all get-out. "That's what I thought."

With a final kiss to my shaft, he pulled my briefs and shorts up, tucked me in, and then zipped and buttoned before he picked my bag up from where he'd dropped it beside him and got to his feet.

"Tease," I said with a smile.

He cupped my cheek and rubbed his thumb over my upper lip. "You need to eat and we're outside. Let's go back to the warehouse and then we can take up where we left off." I flicked my tongue out and licked his thumb. He groaned. "Be careful, baby, or I'll take you again right here, and I'm not liable to stop until you're unconscious."

I shivered.

He threw his head back and laughed, a deep, joyous sound that felt like a rare treat. "You are something else, little wolf." The expression on his face when he looked at me was equal parts amazed and fond, like he was surprised by what he'd found, but pleased too. "Come on." He returned his arm to its spot around my shoulders and led us back to the warehouse.

CHAPTER 12

"Uh, how long have you lived there?" I asked as we walked, hoping it didn't sound like an insult to his den. I wondered whether he'd allow me to make some changes to the space so it wouldn't be so spare. A lamp or two would be nice too, though my night vision had strengthened to the point where I didn't necessarily need light.

"Not long. We've only been in Kfarkattan a few weeks."

That made sense. Word of vampires moving into Kfarkattan had started springing up in Miancarem a couple of weeks prior. And there was no way the elders would have missed their scent for long. Though we didn't, as a rule, spend much time in town, we couldn't avoid regular trips for supplies and such. Hearing that Miguel was new to the area gave me hope that he'd be open to some changes in his living accommodations.

"So, uh, how do you like it so far?" I asked.

"It's fine. Too small for us like it is, but fine."

I furrowed my brow in confusion, trying to work out what he meant.

"What do you mean?" I finally asked.

"We need to stay in more populated areas," he explained,

like it was the most obvious thing on earth. "Even with only seven of us here, the humans will notice us eventually. This town is small enough that they recognize newcomers. Plus, with seven vampires feeding in this limited pool, hangovers and flus will become too common to make sense. Humans see what they want to see, but they're not dumb. We can't stay hidden here for long. At least not right now."

"They get the flu from you?" I asked.

He grinned and massaged my nape. "No, but when they lose blood, they feel a little weaker. It's natural to try to think of a cause that makes sense in their reality. So they blame the flu or think they had too much to drink the night before."

I thought about what he'd said. It didn't match up to my own experience with Miguel feeding from me. "Do all humans feel sick after a vampire feeds from them?" I asked.

"Yes," Miguel said and then paused. "But some of them like it, seek it out, even. And they recover quickly. Uh, unless we take too much."

He sounded ashamed, or at least remorseful, about that last part, so I knew he was talking about himself. I stopped walking and squeezed his upper arm. "When you drank from me, it felt amazing," I told him.

He gave me a weak smile. "That's because we were having sex at the same time, wolf. Sex is meant to feel good."

I refused to let myself think about whether Miguel had had sex with the humans he'd fed from over the years. Refused.

"It did feel good," I said. "You felt good. But what I

meant was that I felt stronger after you fed from me. You said the humans feel weaker after they lose blood. I didn't."

He kissed my forehead. "You're a gift," he murmured against my skin, and I knew I'd distracted him from the reminder of the dark times when he'd taken more than he should have from humans. Truth be told, I didn't want to think about those times, either, because someone else had been doing for my mate what was only mine to do. "I don't deserve you," he whispered, and he nuzzled the soft skin behind my ear.

Once he pulled back, I shrugged and winked at him, trying to lighten the mood, to make him feel good. "You keep touching me the way you been and we'll call it even."

He squeezed me tightly.

"You can count on it, wolf."

We kept walking then, a comfortable silence between us, until I played his words over in my mind. His explanation of why vampires couldn't make a home in Kfarkattan made sense. So much so that it should have been obvious to me. Did that mean he'd be leaving town?

"Miguel?" I said.

"Yeah?"

"What you said about Kfarkattan not being populated enough and you not being able to stay here for long...what does that mean? Don't you live here? I mean, are you—" I took in a deep breath. "Are we leaving town?"

"Live here?" He sounded genuinely surprised. "You thought I lived..." His words trailed off, and he stopped walking and looked at me. "I have a mattress on the floor of a tiny room in a dilapidated warehouse. When you said you were going to stay with me, I thought you understood." He licked his lips nervously. "I thought you knew I was just passing through Kfarkattan. I'm here to buy land so I can come back after they're all done building up the town. But it takes years, sometimes decades, before a growing city is populated enough for my kind to live in it." He shook his head. "So, yeah, I was planning to leave."

It was funny, the things you could figure out without the words being said. I knew, just as surely as I was standing there, that Miguel would stay in Kfarkattan if I asked him. We'd only just met and obviously he had a whole life somewhere else, so that sounded right crazy, I reckon. But seeing the way he looked at me...well, I just knew.

I'd only left the area a few times in my life, and always to visit other packs. Being off pack lands was hard, but at least in Kfarkattan I was in a somewhat familiar setting. Plus, I was walking distance from my family. But frightened though I was, I wouldn't ask Miguel to stay there. I'd meant what I'd said to him—he was now my home. And I was going to buck up and stand by that statement, even if it meant leaving everything and everyone I'd ever known.

"Great," I said, aiming for light and breezy, though my shaking voice and trembling torso probably gave me away as out of kilter and downright terrified. "Where're we going?"

He took my chin in his hand and tipped my head up so our eyes met. "Are you sure?" he asked.

I didn't need to ask what he meant. I knew. Was I sure about leaving the only home I'd ever known? That was what he was asking.

"You're my home now," I answered, repeating what I had already said. "So, uh, tell me where we live."

He searched my eyes, looking for the truth in my words. Once he seemed satisfied, he took my hand in his and kept walking.

"I move around every couple of decades," he said. "We all do. If we stay in the same place for too long, the humans begin to recognize us and then they notice that we don't age. It's easier to leave before that happens. And, if we want, we can come back once we're forgotten."

"Oh," I said, taken aback by the idea of leaving den after den, of never setting down roots.

"I own several places," he said. "I can tell you about them, tell you where they are, and you can choose where we go next. How's that sound, baby?"

With his voice so soft and his expression so tender, it couldn't sound anything but good.

"It sounds perfect," I said as we turned the corner to go into the warehouse. "So, uh, you said you couldn't live in Kfarkattan until they did some building. What kind of building are you waiting on before you can add it to your rotation?" I asked, trying to keep my tone neutral.

"Usually I like to buy land that'll be used as a cemetery. People don't tend to build over cemeteries and they're quiet, especially at night. It's a good way to stay secluded, even when the surrounding city is full of hustle and bustle."

I wasn't sure whether he was making a joke. I mean, I'd heard about vampires living in crypts and coffins, but I figured those were just fables. Miguel's expression held no hint of humor.

"You *live* in cemeteries?" I asked disbelievingly.

Miguel chuckled. "Yes, I do. But it's not like what you're imagining. We can build a really nice, uh, den. It'll have all the modern amenities." He paused. "Well, most of the modern amenities. I'd like to limit the windows. There are a few different places plotted out for cemeteries. Do you want to help me choose?"

"Uh, yes, sure." I wasn't clear on what I'd be able to contribute to any decision making, but I liked that Miguel wanted to include me.

We had entered the warehouse and were walking toward the door leading to the lower level that held Miguel's bed when we heard footsteps rushing toward us.

"Miguel! Hold up."

Miguel stopped, and I followed his lead, trying to swallow down my fear.

Ted, the vampire from the other night, came into view, a few other vampires behind him. Miguel stepped in front of me, not hiding my presence, but putting his body between me and the other vampires.

Ted's eyes widened and he moved his gaze from Miguel to me and back again. "I thought you killed the wolf," he said.

"I thought you were going out hunting," Miguel

snapped back, not addressing Ted's comment.

"We were." Ted gulped and looked over his shoulder at the other vampires. There were three of them, and every single one was staring at me with his mouth hanging open. He turned back to Miguel. "We are. I thought you might want to come with us, so we waited for you."

"I'm fine," Miguel said. "Go ahead."

Ted slowly walked toward us. "Miguel, what's going on? Why is that shifter still here?"

I could see Miguel's muscles tightening. "Ethan is with me," he said gruffly.

"Ethan?" Ted asked.

"The shifter," Miguel clarified. "He's with me."

"Well, shit, don't you know you're not supposed to name stray dogs?" Ralph, the vampire who had led the attack against my mate, said as he walked into the room and headed straight over to Ted. "That'll just make you get attached to them."

My mate clenched his hands into fists and started leaning forward. "Don't you dare talk about him that way!" he shouted. I put my hand on his shoulder, hoping to stop him from fighting over me. Miguel took in a deep breath, seeming to calm down a fair bit. "I want him out of here," he said to Ted.

"What do you mean?" Ted asked.

"I mean your asshole friend isn't welcome," Miguel answered. "Get him out of here today."

"You can't tell me where to go," Ralph scoffed.

Miguel slowly turned his head and glared at the smaller vampire. "I rented this warehouse. Me. Not you, not Ted. I told Ted he could stay here, and I was nice enough to let him bring some friends. My mistake. One I'm going to rectify right away." It looked like Ralph was going to respond, but Miguel was done with him, which he made clear with his body language when he looked away and addressed Ted again. "I'm going downstairs. If I see him in my space when I come back up, you won't like the consequences."

"Miguel, be reasonable," Ted said desperately. "Sunlight's in a few hours. How is he supposed to find a place to go this fast?"

"That's not my problem," Miguel said as he turned around and wrapped his arm over my shoulder, then began leading us toward the basement door.

"You're kicking me out because of a dog?" Ralph asked incredulously.

I flinched, already knowing those words were not a wise choice. Really, the man seemed to have no capacity to learn.

Miguel was across the room, leaning over Ralph, in the blink of an eye. "I told you not to talk about him that way!" He picked the vampire up by the throat and threw him across the wide open space. I raised my eyebrows in surprise at that display of strength, and based on the shocked expressions on the other men's faces, I knew I wasn't alone. Miguel was bigger than Ralph, sure enough, but seeing him toss the man around as if he were nothing but a child's toy was surreal.

My mate wove his fingers together and pulled his hands up, cracking his knuckles. "Consider that a final warning," he said. "Next time I won't be so nice."

I didn't say a word, just stood in place until Miguel got back to me and led me to the basement. He opened the door, waited for me to go through, and then locked it behind us. We walked together in silence and were halfway down the stairs when Miguel took in a sharp breath. "Crap, I didn't even think about how dark it is in here," he said as he wrapped his arm around my waist and slowed our progress. "Are you able to see at all, baby?"

I chuckled nervously, still recovering from the scene in the other room. "Yes, I can see fine." I blinked and looked around, really focusing. "Actually, I can see much better than usual. I noticed it earlier and figured it was because I'd shifted, but I don't remember my kin having night vision this good, even in wolf form."

He furrowed his brow and I could tell he was giving thought to what I'd said. "That's good," he finally said. "Interesting, but good." We reached the bottom of the stairs, and I noticed several containers on the small table I'd seen earlier. The papers that had been on it when I left were stacked neatly on the floor. "I got you some food," Miguel said as he pointed to the table. "I'll get this out too." He tipped his head toward the bag containing the purchases I'd made.

Just thinking about eating made me salivate and my stomach growled loudly. "Sorry," I said with a blush and wondered if he could see my reddened cheeks in the dark.

Miguel finished unpacking the bag, and then he tangled his fingers in my hair, pulled me forward, and planted a quick kiss on my forehead. "I'm the one who's sorry. I should have seen to feeding you earlier."

"It's okay," I said as I sat down. "I'm grown. I can take care of myself."

I noticed his mouth twitching as he pushed some food in front of me. It was like he was trying to hold back a smile. I supposed it was sort of silly, getting defensive about my age with a man who'd been alive for over four centuries.

I sighed deeply. "Look, I'm never going to be as experienced as you, but I'm not aiming to drag you down. I'll carry my own weight."

"Hey." Miguel cupped my cheek. "Nobody accused you of being a drag. I just meant that I'm counting on you to keep me fed now, right?" He pressed his lips to mine. "Seems only fair for me to return the favor."

It was hard to argue with that logic so I grunted in agreement. He grinned again and pulled away. My stomach growled.

"Let's take a break from the talking," Miguel said. "You need to eat."

My stomach growled again, effectively proving his point. I reached for some chicken and stuffed it into my mouth.

Miguel chuckled and sat next to me. "It'll be easier once we move into one of my houses," he said. "We can keep food stocked for you. We'll be on a normal schedule. Everything'll feel more settled."

I nodded and kept eating. Once the first piece of chicken went down, I realized I was more than just a little hungry. Miguel watched me for some time, not saying anything, just looking at me with a small smile on his face, his eyes warm and expression relaxed. Eventually, he stretched across the floor and reached for the papers I'd see on the table.

"Keep right on eating."

I paused midchew and looked at him, trying to gauge whether he was teasing me.

"No, really," he said and then laughed. "It's a pleasure to watch you. I haven't really watched anyone eat in…a very long time."

Not sure how to respond, I grunted again and kept shoveling food into my mouth.

Miguel pushed his chair back and managed to clear off a bit of space on the table. Between the edge of the table, his lap, and the area between the two, he was able to prop up the maps.

"All right, so while you're eating, you can help me choose which piece of land to buy. I'll show you the areas I think will work for a cemetery."

We didn't do things like the humans. Pack lands were more fluid. Shifters built their dens and shops with the Alpha's permission, but, otherwise, we could choose our own location at any time. We didn't buy land in advance and, actually, as I thought about it, I didn't know if pack members bought land at all.

Plus, when our kin passed, we put them to rest in the woods, deep in the earth with the trees sheltering them. So I was having trouble following what Miguel was telling me about buying land today that would be used as an organized burial space for humans in the future. Sure, I was familiar with the concept of a cemetery and he'd explained why he liked living in them, but I still didn't truly understand.

I swallowed down the food in my mouth. "You're buying a cemetery so you can build a house on it?"

Miguel laughed. "No. It doesn't work that way. We can't build a house on a cemetery that already exists because the humans would notice. So when I hear that a city is at the planning stages of growth, I go in, buy land that will work for a cemetery, and then build it. That way, I can make sure that my living space"—Miguel paused—"our living space, is part of the original design. We buy land now, and if the city's plans work, businesses move into the area, which means more humans. A lot of humans in one area means a steady food source for vampires." He angled the map in my direction. "The government is selling off all sorts of land in and around Kfarkattan, which is why we're here. We pick a parcel or two, find someone to set up and run a cemetery, and make sure we build in a caretakers' cottage or a large underground crypt." His gaze met mine. "Does that make sense?" he asked.

Did it make sense? There'd been a whole lot of new things thrown in my direction over the past week. I supposed it made as much sense as the rest.

I shrugged. "As much as it could, I reckon."

"Good enough," Miguel said with a chuckle. He pointed at the map. "So the dark line is the edge of what they have planned to be the main part of Kfarkattan, and the shaded areas show the land that's being sold." He pointed to an area that was circled. "This is the first spot—"

I gasped, lost my grip on the apple I'd just picked up, and dropped it onto the table. "Wait," I said.

Miguel tore his gaze from the map to my face. "What's wrong?" he asked, making me realize I must have sounded as upset as I felt.

"You said the dark line is the edge of Kfarkattan." I tapped my finger on the map. "That there's Miancarem, right inside the dark line." I looked up and met his eyes. "And it's shaded. But that can't be right. Them humans can't expand their city into our pack lands. They can't *sell* our pack lands." I gulped nervously. "Can they?"

CHAPTER 13

"WELL," Miguel said, drawing the word out like he was trying to formulate his response. "The owner of the land can sell it at any time. If the pack set up house someplace they shouldn't be—"

"Shouldn't be?" I shouted, interrupting him. "How can the humans say the pack shouldn't be there? How can they just take it over? Make it part of Kfarkattan? Miancarem's been our pack lands for generations!" I slammed my finger on the map as I spoke.

Miguel pursed his lips and sighed deeply. "Now, you see? That's the problem with shifters. Always thinking they're better than everyone else, that their way is the only way. Well, there are rules about where people can build houses. Shifters can't just go around taking what they want if it already belongs to someone else. But that's exactly what they do because they think humans are so inferior that they can be ignored. But humans greatly outnumber shifters, they outnumber vampires. And it's that kind of superior, arrogant—"

My jaw dropped and whatever appetite I had left deserted me. "You're saying I'm superior and arrogant and...

and…and I think I'm better than everyone else?" The hurt was clear from my tone.

"No, not you," Miguel said in a rush. He leaned toward me and took my hand in his, kissing my palm. "Of course I didn't mean you."

I took a deep breath to calm myself and waited until our eyes met before speaking again. "I am a shifter, Miguel. I'm a mite different from the others, I suppose. And I'm your mate, so I'm leaving my pack. But that don't change who I am. No matter how far away you take me, I will always be a shifter, hear? And I'm right proud of that. I'm not saying my kind's perfect; nobody is. But there ain't nothing wrong with valuing family and community, with setting down roots. Taking care of our own don't make us arrogant or…or superior."

He scoffed. "You're saying shifters consider humans to be equal? Half-souls. That's what shifters call them. Because only shifters have complete souls." His final words were dripping with sarcasm. "That belief in their superiority is arrogance, pure and simple. And it's been the death knell for many a pack."

Miguel had answered his own question, and I couldn't dispute it. But neither was I willing to agree with him. It didn't sit right, bad-mouthing my own, my pack.

"And I suppose you're saying your kind are different?" I snapped. "At least we leave the humans in peace. We're not out attacking them during the night."

"No, you're just out attacking us!" He shoved his chair

back and it tumbled to the ground. "Isn't that right, Ethan? I mean, we met when you and your little friends decided to seek *us* out. We didn't come to your precious pack lands. No, just like all the shifters, you sought us out. And why? Because shifters have decided that vampires aren't worthy of being alive."

He was right and I knew it, but my blood was boiling and the need to defend my kind was all I could feel.

"It's no different than what you do to the humans. Don't forget that I done saw you. You sought them out, attacked them, *hurt* them." I was hitting below the belt and I realized it the moment I saw Miguel flinch. It was as if I could *feel* his reaction to my words—his shame, his pain. Immediately regretting having hurt my mate, I reached my hand out to him. "I'm sorry. I didn't mean—"

"It's okay," Miguel said. But the sorrow rolling off him told me it was anything but okay. "I know you've seen me at my worst. It isn't always like that, though." He paused and furrowed his brow, looking lost in thought. "Actually, it's almost never like that. We need the humans to survive, so we don't aim to hurt them, not really. They're a part of us; their blood runs through our veins. And, don't forget, we started out as humans, all of us, before we were turned. Also, like I already told you, some humans like how they feel after we've fed from them. They seek us out." He dropped his gaze and chewed on the side of his lip. When he spoke again, it was quieter. "Most vampires can usually get by feeding every two or three months, depending on how much they take. And it doesn't have to be enough to really hurt the human. It's been different for me in recent times, harder to control. I need more blood than the others. But no matter how much I take, it's never enough."

"It is now," I said. "You weren't hungry after you drank from me. That's what you said," I said, trying to soothe the pain I'd caused, and also wanting to remind him that he belonged to me now.

"Yes, that's right."

"Well, there you go, then. They weren't enough for you, the humans, and I am. I'm a part of you now. It's *my* blood running through your veins."

Miguel beamed and reached for me. "Come here, wolf," he said as he picked his chair up, settled in it, and patted his thighs.

I got up off my seat and went to my mate. He clasped my waist, those big hands reminding me of his strength and power, which made my breath catch in my throat and my heart quicken. Without saying another word, he pulled me down so I was straddling his lap, our groins pressed together, my backside on his thick, muscular thighs. Then he pushed one hand under my shirt, rubbed circles on my back, and combed the other through my hair.

"Are we through fighting?" he asked me.

"I wasn't fighting none," I mumbled disgruntledly and dropped my chin.

"No?" He tangled his fingers in the hair on the back of my head and tugged until my eyes met his. "My mistake."

He stared at me, his gaze unwavering, eyes unblinking.

"I want to kiss you," I said breathlessly, the need sudden and powerful.

"I'm all yours, wolf," he replied, the words designed to ramp me up further.

We leaned toward each other, and our mouths met in the middle, lips tugging, tongues tangling. I relaxed in his lap, rested against his broad chest, draped my arms over his wide shoulders, and combed my fingers through his silky hair.

"Mmm," I sighed after several long minutes of necking. "I like kissing you."

He cupped my cheek and kissed the tip of my nose. "You're good at it."

"Yeah?" I gave him a small smile. "I'm glad."

Miguel peered into my eyes. He furrowed his brow. "You're still upset," he said.

"Not at you," I assured him. "But"—I flicked my gaze over the map—"my pack lives in Miancarem, my family."

"Yeah," he said, and then he took in a deep breath. "But you don't live there anymore." He took my chin in his hand and held me still, locking his gaze on mine. "Right?"

I trembled. He'd pushed me away from the moment I'd met him, and right then, it felt like he was pulling me closer. It felt good.

"Yes."

"All right, then. You're leaving anyway, so it doesn't matter who owns that land."

I cocked my head to the side and furrowed my brow. I

was confused by his reaction. "'Course it matters," I said. "It don't rightly matter if I live there or not. My pack is there, Miguel. My family."

He stared at me, and I could tell he was thinking about what I'd said, trying to figure it out. Did he not have family? Was that why he didn't understand? As I thought about it, I realized I didn't know much about vampires. Mostly I'd heard stories about vampires being immoral, heard they fixated on the carnal, that they had no sense of loyalty or commitment. I knew they couldn't be in the sun, knew they fed on human blood but were allergic to shifter blood, and knew they were skilled fighters. 'Course one of those things hadn't turned out to be true. At least not when it came to my mate and my blood.

"Miguel?"

"Yeah."

"Do you, uh—" I gulped and licked my lips, trying to figure out how to ask about his past without causing him pain. "Do you have family?"

"No," he answered simply.

I thought that'd be it, that he wasn't going to say no more. And based on his expression, the hardness in his eyes, I reckoned that was how I'd need to leave it. I wanted to know more about my mate, sure enough, but it'd come in time. Or it wouldn't. I'd be able to deal with either outcome. I had him and he wasn't fixin' to leave me behind. That was the only thing that meant anything. I held him tight, rested my head on his shoulder, buried my face into his neck, and inhaled his scent. He smelled right fine.

"I had a family once, obviously," he said, catching me off guard after many long minutes of silence. "But they died a long time ago. Before I was turned. Except for my youngest sister. She lived. Had a son and a granddaughter, even. But Sheila was killed young, and our line ended with her."

My heart ached for him, for the pain he must have endured after losing all his kin. "I'm sorry," I rasped, my throat thick with emotion.

"Nothing to be sorry about," he answered, his voice clear and strong, showing no indication that we were talking about something horrible, tragic. "It was a very long time ago. Before even your great-grandparents were born." He chuckled darkly. "Hell, it was long past that."

I kissed his neck tenderly. "I'm still sorry, Miguel," I said. He shrugged and grunted. "I have a sister too," I added, figuring I should share with him if I expected him to share with me. "She has five boys. Just the other day, she told me she's expecting again. She's right certain it'll be a girl this time. Two, actually. Twins."

"She's the one I scented?" he asked. "That night in the alley, after you were gone. She's the one who came for you?"

I nodded. "Yes. That was Crissy. She left pack lands without anybody knowing, not even her husband. She came all on her own to collect me and take me on home to Miancarem." I tipped my head back and met his gaze. "She's strong, my sister. Special."

Miguel met my gaze and something passed in his eyes,

emotions I couldn't recognize.

"I can't fix things for them if they insist on thumbing their noses at the humans," he said eventually. "But if they're willing to cooperate with them, to work in the system, I can help them keep their land. I can probably even manage to create a barrier between Miancarem and Kfarkattan, enough that the pack lands will never be a highly populated city."

"Really?" I sat up straight and felt the tightness in my chest loosen. "You can do that?"

"Not me. Them. I said I can *help* them. I can't do it for them, Ethan. If those shifters can't learn to live in the world, they won't be living a generation from now. I've been around a long time. When I was your age there were twice as many packs as there are now. Did you know that?"

Know? Probably not. But I'd heard tale of packs that weren't around no longer. Actually... "I've heard folks say vampires came after some packs. Burned down dens, schools. That's why the pack don't want vampires around, why we try to scare them away when they come near. We're just defending—"

"Bullshit," he snapped. I stayed silent, waiting for an explanation. I was starting to get to know my mate, starting to understand that his reactions were a mite rough, that it took him a bit to share, but share he would. "That's yet another ridiculous story shifters came up with to justify their actions. We have no reason to go after them. I was there, Ethan. Maybe not for every pack, but for enough of them to know why they're gone. More humans came and the land changed around them. The shifters refused to adapt. Some took to their animal forms. Others fled. Vampires had no part in it. We stayed away." He closed his eyes and shook his head, disgust clear on his face. "We mind our own business. But like I told you, we need the humans, we *were* humans. When the shifters decided to destroy everything around them, when they went after the humans, burning down buildings and trees, thinking that'd keep the humans away, vampires stopped them. We didn't go looking for a fight. That's the shifter way, not ours. If anybody was defending, it was us. Vampires defended humans. We defended the land shifters said they considered precious until somebody else wanted it. That was us, the soulless bloodsuckers. *Us.*"

My brain raced, trying to catch up to what Miguel said, to his version of events. It was too much to process at once, too horrible to be possible. And yet, there was enough familiarity there to make me pause before I denied it outright. What would my kind do if our pack lands were threatened by the humans? How would we respond? Would we behave exactly like Miguel said? A cold shiver racked my body. I didn't want to find out.

"Will you help us?" I beseeched him. "Please?"

"You don't need to beg me, baby," he said, losing that hard edge he'd had just moments prior. "I'll try to help your kind." I'd breathed a sigh of relief and opened my mouth to thank him when he cupped my cheeks and pierced me with his gaze. "But listen to me carefully. If they don't listen, if they start to fight, they're on their own. I'm taking you and leaving this town, leaving this state, maybe the nation. We will be long gone before they can get to you."

"They won't," I insisted, shaking my head. "Shifters protect our own. My pack might not understand me, but they won't hurt me."

He scoffed but didn't dispute my words, at least not out loud. "Even if you're right that they won't go after you physically, staying here and watching what a pack can do to itself, how they can destroy everything they claim to hold dear... Watching what can happen to your family—" He shook his head and gulped, deep pain flashing for a moment in his dark eyes. "I won't let them hurt you. I'll try to help them, but if they refuse, we're leaving."

I couldn't respond; there was simply too much emotion coursing through me. Fear, sure enough. I was afraid for my kin, afraid for my pack, afraid for myself. But also there was a joy so profound it warmed me to my core. Miguel might write off our pack history and how we were made as an absurd superstition. He might dispute the concept of true mates. But his actions, his feelings, showed me all I needed to know. What I felt for my mate was being reflected right back at me, just as strong, just as sure.

"Ethan?" he said, bringing my attention back to our conversation. "Do you understand?"

"Yes," I answered. With as much as I didn't know in that moment, I understood everything of consequence.

CHAPTER 14

"I DON'T like it," Miguel said in that tone he had that sounded like a growl, which was surprising from a man who wasn't part wolf.

My vampire was cuter than a sack full of puppies when he was ornery and protective. I couldn't keep the grin off my face about that last bit.

"You think this is funny, Ethan? Well, it isn't. You've been gone for several days. And even though we scrubbed you clean, you still smell like me. I don't understand it but those shifters are bound to notice."

"'Course I smell like you. We're mated. You ain't gonna wash that off. I didn't realize that was why you were so, uh, thorough in the bath."

My mate pulled me into his arms and nuzzled my throat. "It wasn't the only reason I was thorough," he whispered.

I couldn't hold back the tremble. That bath had been like no other I'd experienced. Miguel had caressed every inch of my skin, outside and in, his strong hands slick with water and soap. Lord, that had felt good, my mate exploring me deep inside with a finger while he kissed me and milked my erection, not stopping until my knees were weak and I could barely breathe. I moaned at the memory and turned my head, aiming for Miguel's mouth.

He sucked my bottom lip between his and licked it. I crowded against him, rubbing my swollen prick on his thigh.

"Miguel," I moaned.

He wrapped his arms around me, cupped my backside, and then, suddenly, he jumped back. "Damn it!" he shouted, panting. "I can't stop touching you and it's only making my scent all over you stronger."

I sighed. "That's not...the scent isn't from you touching me. It's just my scent now that we're mated. That there's how it works." I could tell from his expression that he didn't understand what I meant. "That's what happens with true mates. Once we tied, our scents wove together so we smell the same but different."

"The same, but different?"

"Yes." I nodded and stepped closer to him, so we were touching again. "My scent is still there, right? So I smell like me but I smell like you too. Your scent changed too. You smell like me now."

"Shit," Miguel said as he shook his head in frustration.

"What's the matter?" I asked. "Is it so bad to share my scent?"

I didn't realize how naïve and pathetic that question would sound until after I'd already asked it. The things I considered romantic probably struck my four-hundred-year-old mate as silly. Like sharing something as elemental as our scents. Or having him smell of me so nobody could doubt my claim on him.

"No, baby." That deep voice washed over me, and I looked up, meeting Miguel's gaze. "I didn't realize our scents had changed, didn't know something like that was possible, but I'm not upset about it. Actually..." He turned up one side of his mouth in a wicked grin. "I like the idea that you smell like me, like I've marked you so completely. But I can't let you go onto pack lands now. I've seen what shifters do to vampires. It isn't safe."

"I'm not a vampire, and I swear, shifters never hurt our own. I'll be safe. Besides, I don't have a choice. I need to talk to Crissy, set up a meeting so we can explain about the pack lands being sold."

"Fine," Miguel said, agreeing too easily. "Then I'll go with you." He took a step toward the woods that made up the edge of Miancarem.

I grasped his arm. "You know you can't go onto pack lands, Miguel. It'd be considered an act of aggression."

"A walk in the woods is considered aggression, and you *actually* think shifters aren't the cause for the violence between our kinds?" he said sarcastically.

I wasn't going to get into another debate with him about who was at fault for the divide between vampires and shifters. I wasn't sure either of us had the answer. And, besides, it was a pointless argument.

"Whatever the cause, that's how things are now," I said. "But we're aiming to fix it, right?"

"Fix what? I'm not on some goodwill mission

representing vampires, Ethan. Even if I wanted to do that, I can't speak for anyone but myself. No vampire can. We don't have packs and Alphas. We have autonomy and personal responsibility and—" He sighed deeply and stopped ranting, probably realizing that line of talking would end in an argument. "Besides, that's not what I want to do. I just want to make sure you don't lose your family like..." He trailed off and closed his eyes for a few beats. "I can't keep you safe if you go onto pack lands without me," he said softly.

"I'll go straight to Crissy's den and back," I assured him. "It won't take me but two shakes of a lamb's tail."

"A wolf making sheep references," Miguel said with a roll of his eyes. "Will wonders never cease?" I didn't think he expected an answer to that question, so I didn't give him one. "All right. You go to your sister's house, no pit stops. You tell her where to meet us tomorrow night, then you come right back to me."

I put my hands on his shoulders and stretched up until our lips touched. "Always," I whispered. "I'll always come back to you."

He threaded his fingers in my hair and pulled me closer, then tilted his face and pressed his mouth against mine roughly, teeth nibbling, tongue licking until I opened for him. Then he pushed his tongue past my lips, thrusting and tasting, devouring. By the time he released me, my lungs were heaving and my shaft was throbbing.

"I'll give you an hour, wolf," he said. "One hour. Then I'm coming after you."

I nodded and then walked into the woods in the direction of Crissy's den. Though it surely wasn't possible, I felt like my mate's gaze was glued to me even when the thick brush and trees had me hidden from view. It was comforting, the idea of Miguel watching me. I laughed internally at how crazy that sounded—a shifter comforted by the idea of a vampire following his every move.

But it was true. I felt comfortable with Miguel. Comfortable and safe and right. Seeing as how I'd never felt right around nobody, myself included, that was really saying something. It was like the man had been made for me, or, considering he'd been walking the earth long before I was born, it was more accurate to say I'd been made for him. Or maybe we were made for each other. Whatever the words, the point was clear. And, as if in direct reaction to my thoughts of my mate, my blood pounded through my veins, stronger, faster, louder. I wanted to feel his breath on my skin, his fangs piercing my veins, his mouth drawing out my blood in long, hard pulls.

Come back to me. I heard his words in my head, or maybe I felt them in my heart. Either way, I quickened my pace, anxious to finish my errand so I could return to my mate.

Strong as I was now that I'd mated, it didn't take me long to get to Crissy's den. I ran fast, the exertion feeling good whereas before it would have hurt my limbs. The slap of branches against my skin barely registering whereas before the touch of anything was akin to a burn. The change was amazing and all because of the long-haired man waiting for me, the man who didn't want to let me go. I smiled, feeling pleased as punch, and quickened my pace.

Shortcuts kept me off the main roads and allowed me to reach my destination faster. And before I knew it, I was standing in front of my sister's door.

The door swung open before I could knock. "Ethan!" Crissy hissed as she yanked me inside and closed the door behind me. She wrapped her arms around my waist and hugged me tightly. The silence lasted but a few seconds and then the barrage of questions started. "After I got your note, I didn't count on seeing you none for a long spell. Is everything okay with your mate? What're you doing back here on pack lands? Nobody saw you, right? Are you hungry? Thirsty? Tired? Let's sit down." She pulled me toward the couch and sat next to me, taking my hands in hers. "Tell me everything, right quick," she said excitedly.

I didn't have time right then to catch her up on everything I'd learned and experienced in the short time I'd been away. We'd have time for that later, I hoped.

"I can't stay," I said. "I'm here to—" I stopped mid-sentence. "Are the boys in bed?" I asked, not wanting to risk having one of her young overhear our conversation.

"Yes," she answered. "They've been asleep going on an hour."

"Okay." I breathed a sigh of relief. "Good. I need you to come into Kfarkattan tomorrow night. Meet me in that alley where you found me last time. There's some papers you'll want to see, and Miguel needs to explain what the humans have planned."

"Miguel?" she asked.

"My mate," I clarified.

I hadn't told her my mate's name in the note I'd left behind, figuring the paper could get into someone else's hands, and giving anybody information about Miguel would have put him in danger. All right, then. Maybe there was something to my mate's assertions that my kind was a bit hot under the collar.

She leaned in and sniffed me. "You really done found your true mate." Her smile was wide and genuine. "And he really is a vampire. How about that."

I returned her smile, pleased as punch that she could share my joy. "So can you come?" I asked again. "Alone," I clarified. "No one can know about this."

"Of course," she answered.

"Like hell you say." Richie's voice caught us both off guard. I jerked my head toward the hallway and saw my brother-in-law glaring at us, his arms crossed over his chest. "You ain't going into town on your lonesome to meet some bloodsucker."

My heart dropped.

"Fine," Crissy said and met his gaze head on. "Then I reckon you'll be taggin' along."

I didn't argue. Richie was family, and I figured we'd need all the help we could get.

He didn't respond to my sister right away, just stood in

place, not moving a muscle other than the one in his jaw that seemed to have developed a tic. Eventually he gave a sharp nod.

"It's a plan," Crissy said joyfully.

"Good." I squeezed her hand and got up from the couch. "I have to go. Miguel's waiting on me. Tomorrow night, the alley from the other morning, we'll talk more."

"I TOLD my sister we'd meet them in the alley." I cupped my hands on the window and pressed my forehead against them, squinting as I looked past the street outside and over to the alley beyond. We were in an abandoned building across the way from the alley. "They'll never be able to see us all the way over here," I said to Miguel.

"That's the point," Miguel muttered. He had walked over when my back was turned, and as he spoke, he circled his muscular arms around my chest and burrowed his face into my hair. "We'll see them first, so we'll know if they bring reinforcements."

I turned around and traced my mate's shirt collar before grasping it and pulling him down so our eyes were level. "I already told you that it'll just be Crissy and Richie."

"You also told me your sister would be meeting us alone. I didn't hear word one about a husband until after you went over there by yourself. What if he had hurt you?" He'd near about lost his mind the first time I'd mentioned Richie, and now he was getting ramped up all over again. His arms flew in the air as he spoke. "Did you think about that? What if I couldn't get to you in time?"

"Why would he hurt me?"

Miguel shrugged. "How the hell should I know? Those shifters attack for no reason. They can't be trusted. Especially the males."

"*Those* shifters?" I asked as I raised one eyebrow.

"You know what I mean," Miguel muttered.

Strange though it was, I did know what he meant. My mate was worried about me.

"I'm just fine," I told him. "Ain't nobody hurt me none."

Miguel grunted and wrapped his arms around me once more, pulling me close. I straddled his thick muscular thigh, pressed my rapidly expanding prick against him, and rocked just a tad.

"Does that thing ever go down?" he asked with a chuckle. "Because I'm pretty sure you're hard ninety percent of the day."

I blushed and stopped moving. "Sorry," I said as I looked down at my feet, feeling suddenly uncomfortable about my out-of-control hormones. "I'm not usually like this, honest. It's been just since I met you. I can stop, though."

Miguel took my chin between his fingers and tilted it up until my gaze met his. "Only since you met me?" he asked gruffly.

I nodded.

He dipped his head and whispered into my ear. "I like

that, wolf." He swiped his tongue across my lobe and then sucked it into his mouth. "I like that a lot." Then he cupped my backside in those big hands and squeezed tight as he tugged forward, encouraging me to rock again.

"Yeah?" I asked. "'S okay?"

He didn't answer with words, just grunted and shoved one hand down the back of my pants while he worked my zipper open with the other. "What time is your sister supposed to be here?" he asked, his voice as rough as his hand was gentle. He kneaded my backside, fondled the sensitive skin in my crease, and got closer and closer to the puckered hole he seemed to enjoy massaging and penetrating with his thick fingers.

"We didn't set a specific time," I answered in between pants. I cried out when he encircled my erection with his warm hand, and then I thrust forward, desperately seeking friction.

"Good." His voice was husky, his pupils dilated. "Because I need to take care of you before we entertain your family." And with those words, he worked one finger inside me.

"Miguel!" I shouted.

"You like that?" He stroked my hard length faster and pumped his finger within me at the same pace, crooking it just so and touching a spot inside that made me tremble. "I like making you feel good, wolf."

My hips rocked madly as moans and whimpers fell from my mouth. And then, just when I was about to spill my seed, my mate dropped down to a squat and sucked the head of my erection between his lips.

"Ah!" I shouted as I shot over and over again, filling his mouth with my release.

My knees gave out, and I collapsed onto the ground, dropping my head onto Miguel's thighs. My chest heaved as I tried to take in air, and my heart felt like it was pounding strong enough to break my ribs.

When my brain finally regained some function, I realized that the scent of my mate's arousal was strong. The heat from his engorged shaft was close to my lips, separated by the thin layer of cotton he wore. I reached for his button and looked up, asking for approval with my eyes.

He caressed my cheek and graced me with a smile so tender it made my heart skip a beat. "Only if you want to, baby," he said.

I'd been longing to taste him so I dipped my face until my lips were pressed against the bulge in his pants and then I mouthed the fabric-covered hardness as I unfastened his button. I had to pull back long enough to lower his zipper and shove his pants and briefs down over his erection. It was brown and thick and so unbelievably hot. I whimpered as I rubbed my cheek against it, then my lips, and finally my tongue—long swipes intermingled with short laps.

Miguel's breath quickened, and he clutched my shoulders tightly. When I took his crown into my mouth and sucked hard, he gasped and thrust his hips up, pushing himself farther inside.

"Yes, Ethan!" he shouted and then warm fluid splashed onto my tongue, the taste of my mate strong and arousing.

I swallowed and sucked and licked until he pushed my head back and sat on the ground. I climbed right onto Miguel's lap, straddled his hips, and flung my arms over his shoulders. He tangled his fingers in my hair and held my face still as he gazed into my eyes.

"Good?" he asked me.

My nod seemed to give all the assurance he needed. He relaxed and shoved his hand underneath my shirt, then rubbed circles on my back. I rested my head on his shoulder and enjoyed the feel of his strength and warmth.

"Do you hear that?" Miguel asked after some time.

I lifted my head and perked my ears up. "That's my sister," I said.

Miguel took in a deep breath. "It's showtime."

CHAPTER 15

"AND how do we know we'll be safe?" Richie snapped at Miguel. He was standing in front of Crissy, blocking her from our view. "How do we know this here ain't no trap?"

Miguel sneered at him, his dour expression doing nothing to hide the disdain he had for my kind.

"Richie," I said, pulling his attention away from my mate. He jerked his head toward me. "We're all standing in a dark alley right now. If we were going to trap you, wouldn't this be a better place than the diner down the street? Like Miguel explained, we want to go to the diner so we can sit down somewhere lit and show you papers."

I didn't mention that the need for light was for their benefit, not ours. Miguel could see in the dark better than most people could see in the sunlight. And since he had been feeding from me, my night vision had improved along with my energy level and strength.

"Well, iffen y'all wanted to meet at a diner, why didn't you say so in the first place? Why'd you tell us to meet in this here alley?" he asked, completely ignoring the logic I'd just tried to impart.

"Maybe they were worried about a trap too, Richie," my

sister said quietly, likely intending for her words to be heard by her husband alone so his pride wouldn't be damaged.

But I heard her just fine, and based on the small smirk that came and went from Miguel's face right quick, I was guessing he'd heard her too. Along with remarkably good night vision, my hearing was sharp as a tack. My mate had truly healed me.

Feeling unaccountably grateful, I turned to him, pressed my chest to his, and circled my arms around his waist. I forgot for a moment about Richie and Crissy and alleys and maps and thought only of the man in my arms.

"You okay, baby?" he whispered into my ear as he cupped my nape and gave me a supportive squeeze.

"Better than," I answered. "Just wanted to hug you is all."

"Good. You feel free to do that anytime."

"This here vampire is truly your mate?" Richie asked, taking me off guard and tearing my attention back to my surroundings.

"He is," I said proudly. "Miguel is my true mate. We tied together and claimed each other."

Richie flinched, seeming a mite uncomfortable, but then his stance relaxed and he took Crissy's hand in his and stepped closer to us. "All right, then. Let's go to that there diner and take a look at what your mate has to show us," he said.

I smiled and leaned against Miguel, who was still standing behind me. I felt him lower his head and then his hot breath ghosted over my ear. "That's it? We've been standing out here arguing because, like a typical shifter, he wouldn't listen to reason, and now he's suddenly willing to follow us to the diner?" He shook his head and furrowed his brow. "I think he's up to something."

I chuckled and turned around, resting my palm on my Miguel's cheek. "You do realize you sound just as suspicious as Richie, right? He was being careful is all."

"And then all of sudden he changed his mind. Doesn't that strike you as strange?"

"No. It strikes me that he wasn't sure whether I was telling the truth about you being my true mate and now he believes me."

He tilted his head to the side. "And what does that have to do with him changing his mind about going to the diner?"

Richie and Crissy had reached us, and Miguel was no longer talking quietly, so they heard him.

"You're Ethan's mate," Crissy said. "That there makes you family. I'm real pleased to meet you, Miguel."

From the look on Miguel's face, I knew he still wasn't clear on what had changed, but he didn't say anything else. He just wrapped his hand around my elbow and started walking to the diner.

"WAIT, wait. Hold on up for just one minute now," Richie said. He was leaning over the table, his palms flat on the map and his gaze darting around the page. "What do you mean they're fixin' to sell our pack lands?" He looked up from the paper and glared at Miguel. "Who said that there land is theirs to sell? Our pack has been there for generations."

"Who said... They said. They're the government. It doesn't matter if you've been living there. If you don't own the land—"

"What does that even mean?" Richie interrupted. "It's land. Dirt and trees and wind and sky and such. We don't own the land, we share in its gifts."

At that comment, my big, strong, gruff mate rolled his eyes like a put-upon child. "That's a very nice philosophy," he said, though his tone sounded less than sincere. "But that's not how the world works. Land is owned by people, and if they don't want to let anybody else *share in its gifts*, that's their right. So, if your pack wants to keep this land, they need to buy it."

Richie's jaw dropped. "We have to buy our own land?"

"Haven't you been listening to me?" Miguel snapped. "It isn't your land. But it can be. If. You. Buy. It."

A growl rumbled in Richie's chest, and he curled his lips over his teeth. When I noticed him clenching and unclenching his fists, I knew he was trying to restrain his anger. He took in a deep breath and then let it out slowly. "Go on and explain it to me again," he said.

"Please," Crissy added.

I put my hand on Miguel's knee and squeezed it. Then I rubbed his thigh.

"All right," he said. "Here is how it works."

Miguel wasn't as patronizing the second time around. Instead, he put paper after paper in front of Richie and Crissy, showing them maps and price sheets, explaining which land would remain national forestland and which would be private property. He answered their questions patiently, and though it was clear that Richie was distressed, he was no longer glaring at my mate.

"Does the pack have that there kind of money?" Crissy asked her husband.

"Richie's father is one of the pack Betas," I explained to Miguel. "So he has a good handle on finances."

"I don't rightly know," Richie said as he dragged his fingers through his hair. "If we all pool together, we might should be able to buy most of it, like the dens, and probably the school, but—" He gulped and pointed at the map. "The human town will come right up to Miancarem. And I don't think we'll be able to get enough funds to buy the open areas."

"Why is that such a bad thing?" Miguel asked. "Maybe it's time your kind integrated a little better with the humans. If you did more of that, you wouldn't need me to tell you what they plan to do with your town. You can't continue to be so isolated. It's threatening your survival."

"Maybe so," I said. "But how can cubs shift and play if they've got humans as neighbors? How can pack members go for runs or talk openly among themselves? I think you're right about changes being necessary, but the pack can't live among the humans, Miguel." I lowered my voice. "It's like

what you told me about where vampires build their homes,"
I said, referring to his explanation that one of the benefits
of cemeteries was that they were mostly empty, particularly
at night, so vampires had a safe space, away from prying
human eyes.

Crissy chewed on her lip nervously as she looked over
the map once again. Richie scanned the paper that held all
the numbers, his brow furrowed and concern etched on
every line of his face. None of us spoke for several minutes,
the atmosphere tense.

"I'll buy the open areas in Miancarem," Miguel said,
cutting through the silence. "And I'll buy enough land on
the outside of your pack lands to create a sufficient privacy
barrier. But that's all I can do. You'll need to work with your
pack or your Alpha and buy the land that holds your houses
and shops and schools."

Richie flicked his gaze up and squinted at Miguel.
"Why would a bloodsucker do that for our pack?" he asked
suspiciously.

"I wouldn't do shit for your pack," Miguel answered
roughly.

Richie opened his mouth, no doubt to say something
equally kind and diplomatic, but I beat him to the punch.

"Thank you," I said to my mate. "I appreciate it."

Miguel grunted and threw his arm around my
shoulders.

Crissy beamed and put her hand on Richie's bicep.
"He's Ethan's mate, Rich," she said.

My brother-in-law looked at me and clamped his mouth shut, the pieces finally falling together so he understood exactly why my mate was willing to spend his money on land he'd never use.

"Are we done here?" Miguel said more than asked as he pushed his chair back. "We need to get going." He got to his feet and reached his hand out toward me. I stood right up. "You can keep those papers," he said to Crissy and Richie. "I have other copies. Show them to your pack, do whatever you need to do, but act quickly. I'm not the only one interested in buying land in the newly expanding Kfarkattan, and once they start advertising, offers are sure to come pouring in."

And with that, he turned on his heel and walked toward the door.

Crissy scrambled up out of the chair. "Ethan," she said. I went over to her and she hugged me tightly. "Thank you."

"I didn't do nothing," I said as I shrugged.

"Oh, you surely did. If it wasn't for you, our land would be gone. But now we have a chance to save it, to save our pack." She pulled back and gazed into my eyes. "You done that, little brother."

I shook my head. "Not me. Miguel."

"Crissy's right," Richie said. "That there vampire is helping us because he's your mate. No other reason."

"That's right," Crissy said. "So you see? You're saving us." Her eyes clouded and suddenly she was looking through me. "And this here is only the beginning, my special brother, just the beginning."

"Ethan," Miguel called to me.

I looked back over my shoulder. "Coming," I said to him. I kissed Crissy's cheek and squeezed her one last time, happy to see that her eyes had cleared. Then I rushed over to Miguel.

"You take care of my brother, hear!" Crissy shouted after us.

Miguel clutched my elbow and pulled me up against his side. He turned back to look at my sister. "That's not something you ever need to doubt," he said. And then he led us out the door.

"MIGUEL?" I whispered later that night when we were in bed, naked, our sated bodies curled together. He was on his back, and I lay on his chest, alternately licking and sucking on his brown nipples.

"Mmm," he answered as he stroked my hair with one hand and massaged my nape with the other.

"How is it you can buy all that land on your own, but according to Richie, our whole pack combined doesn't have the funds to do it?"

"Because unlike those shifters, I pay attention to the world around me and I realize the bartering system is a thing of the past."

Though I didn't understand exactly what he was saying, the fact that it was intended as an insult to my pack was clear. I flattened my palms on either side of his torso and pushed myself up so I could look into his eyes. I conveyed my disapproval without words.

His expression softened immediately and he pulled me back down against his chest. "I'm sorry, baby," he said, kissing my head and petting my backside. "There's no reason for me to bark at you."

I snorted.

"You think that's funny, do you?" he asked, amusement clear in his tone. "A barking vampire."

My shoulders shook and I grinned at my mate. "Yes, I surely do find it funny."

Miguel returned my smile and leaned up so he could kiss my forehead.

"I know you were raised on your pack lands and you probably don't have a clear picture of the human world, but people earn money and they use it to buy land and goods and services. Then the people who provide those items use the same money to buy things for themselves. But shifters aren't like that. They barter within their pack and with other packs."

"We don't barter," I corrected.

"Don't you?" he asked, as he arched one eyebrow. "What would you call it, then? You have pack members who grow produce. They give it to other pack members who teach at the schools where they send their kids. Or maybe to pack members who raise cattle or chickens. And those pack members provide eggs and milk and beef in exchange for clothing from pack members who sew. Am I right?"

He was, sort of. "It isn't quite like that, Miguel. We don't exchange one thing for another. Every member of the pack has a job that provides for the pack. Folks take what they need and give what they have, but it ain't like how you make it sound. We don't barter."

He sighed. "Call it what you want, the point is that shifters deal almost exclusively with other shifters within their packs, and they don't charge each other money for anything. That means very little outside money enters the pack. So when something like this happens, when the shifters are forced to deal with the humans, they're left vulnerable."

"And you're not?" I asked.

"No," he said as he shook his head. "I'm not vulnerable to the human world because I live in the human world. I own businesses that cater to humans. Those cemeteries I told you about are just one example. And any land I buy that I don't end up using for myself, I rent out to others. That's a source of income too. I'm four hundred years old, Ethan. That's a long time to build a nest egg."

I thought about what he said, running the words over in my mind. I had a lot to learn in this new life away from my pack, away from everything and everyone I knew. And though it terrified me, I wasn't going to run from it. But—

Miguel interrupted my impending panic attack. "What are you thinking about that's putting that frown on your face?"

"I don't have a...a nest egg," I told him. "I don't have land or businesses. I have a couple of sets of clothes, a pocketknife, and a box my sister made for me when I was a kid. When I lived on pack lands, that was okay. The pack gave me what I needed, and if I'd been healthy enough, I would have found a calling and I would have contributed to the pack. Now I'm plenty healthy, but I don't have my pack and"—I sighed deeply—"I don't have anything to contribute."

"Sure you do," he said. "You have plenty to contribute."

I looked into his eyes, hoping there was truth to his words. I didn't want to be a drain on my mate, didn't want him to regret having me in his life.

"Like what?" I asked.

He licked the vein in my neck and then sucked on it when it started to pulse stronger. "You're feeding me now, remember? Just you."

I scoffed. "That's as much for me as it is for you, Miguel. I enjoy providing for you in that way. I crave it, even. Plus, I don't want you dipping your toes in somebody else's ocean, so—"

Miguel's deep laugh cut off the rest of my words. His broad chest rumbled beneath me and he held me tight.

"Now, you see there?" he said once his rolling laughter had died down to a light chuckle. "That's what you're contributing. I don't know when I've ever laughed as much as I do with you, wolf. And if you want to do more, I'll teach you what you need to know to help me with the businesses and the land."

"Yeah?" I asked hopefully. "Because I'll work real hard

to learn. I want to help you."

He pushed my hair off my forehead and tenderly pressed his lips to mine. We traded slow and gentle kisses until my eyes felt heavy and my limbs weak. Then I tucked my face into my mate's neck and breathed in his scent as sleep overtook me.

"You've already helped me, Ethan," Miguel whispered quietly. "You've reminded me what it's like to feel."

CHAPTER 16

A WEEK later, our time in Kfarkattan had come to a close. Miguel and Richie had talked again, and Miguel even introduced him to one of the humans responsible for selling off the Miancarem land. Apparently my mate had had other business dealings with this man and favors were owed. Hands were shaken, documents were signed, money changed hands, and by the end, my mate owned a good portion of our pack lands, along with hundreds of acres of abutting property, and the human had promised to sell the rest of Miancarem to a group of investors represented by Richie. Those investors, of course, were the pack members, but Miguel had explained which words the human would understand and which we should avoid using or risk causing confusion.

Though I wouldn't go so far as to say that Richie liked Miguel, I think he had developed a measure of respect for my vampire. Not enough to smile at Miguel or thank him for what he'd done, mind you, but enough to swallow his pride and ask for help, or at least imply that he needed it. And that was what brought us back to the diner for a meeting with Richie.

"We can get close to all the money them humans is asking for the land we're using, but not enough to buy all of it," Richie said. His voice was strained and he was having trouble meeting Miguel's eyes from across the table.

"And by the land you're *using*," Miguel said. "I take it you mean the land with your buildings but not the common areas or the roads, not the land on the outskirts of Miancarem that'll give you a buffer from Kfarkattan."

Richie grunted and gave a sharp nod, then he raised his gaze for a moment before dropping it again. He tapped on the table nervously with one hand and clenched and released the other. His foot seemed to be keeping time with his hand, moving rapidly underneath the table.

Miguel spoke again without waiting on Richie to say more, without forcing the man to grovel. "I'll buy the land holding the shops and the school," he said. "They're adjacent to the common areas, which I already bought, so it'll be just a matter of me taking on a bigger plot. Will that solve the issue?"

"It will," Richie said, disbelief and gratitude both evident in his tone. "We can take care of the rest." He picked up his coffee mug and then looked down and noticed it was empty. "Do either of y'all need a refill?" he asked. Then he looked over to my single cup and seemed to remember that what my mate drank wasn't on a restaurant menu. "Uh, do you need a refill, Ethan?"

"Yes, please." I handed him my mug. "Thank you." I waited until Richie was at the counter, and then I put my hand on Miguel's thigh and leaned close to him. "You're a good man," I said.

"I'm a soulless bloodsucker, remember? Isn't that why Richie keeps meeting us on his own? You have noticed that, right?"

"I have," I said evenly.

"And you realize that's because he hasn't told any of his pack members where he got the information about the land being sold? In fact, I'd guess they still don't know a thing about the common areas because there isn't enough money for the pack to buy them and no way is he going to tell them that a vampire is going to own part of what they consider *their* land."

I sighed. "You're a good man because even though you know all of this, you're still helping them."

"I'm helping you, Ethan. Not anybody else."

"And I appreciate it. But you're helping them too. And you didn't make Richie beg. You're not gloating." I looked into his eyes. "You're a good man, Miguel."

"Here you go." Richie slid the coffee mug in front of me and sat down.

"Listen, uh, Miguel." He looked down at his mug and then back at my mate. "I just wanted to say that—"

"Richie?" an angry voice boomed from behind us. I recognized that voice. It was Richard Smith, Richie's father. From the terrified look on Richie's face, I knew he hadn't told him about our meeting. This was an unfortunate and unexpected development.

I didn't turn around, hoping I wouldn't be noticed. Richie jumped to his feet, no doubt hoping to catch his father where he stood, rather than having the man walk over to us. Neither plan worked.

"I done thought that was you," Mr. Smith said as he approached our table. "I was walking by and I seen you through the window. You didn't tell me you were coming into town. And why are you in this here restaurant instead of home with your..." His eyes widened and he furrowed his brow in confusion. "Ethan?"

Well, all right, then. Apparently crouching low in my seat and gulping down scathing hot coffee in the hope that the mug would block my face hadn't been enough to hide my presence. I set the mug down and looked up to meet the older shifter's gaze. Though I tried to appear calm, I couldn't help but squirm in my seat. That and the crack in my voice surely gave away my anxiety. "Hello, Mr. Smith," I said.

Miguel, bless him, looked right at me, clearly concerned about my change in mood. Then he twisted his body so he was almost completely blocking me and glared up at Richie's father. I knew he was about to speak, and though I wasn't privy to his exact words, I had a strong sense of his emotions and they weren't pretty.

Before the situation could go from bad to worse, I put my hand on Miguel's shoulder and squeezed tight while trying to convey my own feelings to him—a desire for peace with Mr. Smith, with my pack. I didn't rightly know whether it'd work, not ever having been able to communicate with anybody at that level. But I'd heard tale of true mates who could all but read each other's minds, and I hoped that maybe my mate and I had started to develop some of those qualities and he'd be sensitive enough to hear my words without me speaking them aloud.

Though his posture tensed, Miguel held his tongue. I wondered whether that was in reaction to my silent plea.

"What in tarnation is going on here?" Richie's father hissed. He cocked his chin toward Miguel but wouldn't deign to rest his gaze on him. "That there's a bloodsucker," he added, as if that was information Richie and I somehow could have missed. It seemed being quiet didn't make my vampire invisible, so it was too much to hope that Mr. Smith would pay him no mind.

Richie was already standing, so he needed only one step to be next to his father. He put his hand on the older man's shoulder and tried to move him toward the door. "Let's go, Papa," he said.

Unfortunately, it wasn't going to be as easy as leaving the diner and then forgetting what he'd seen.

"I asked you a question, boy," he said as he glared at his son. "What are y'all doing here? And why are you sittin' with a soulless vampire?" He spoke in a low voice, just loud enough for us to hear. For all that it was quiet, the tone was also shocked and angry and repulsed. It was impressive, really, that he'd been able to pack all that emotion into just a few barely audible words. Then, almost as an afterthought, he jerked his face toward me and added, "Get up!"

Richie was a big man, a strong man, and sharp as a tack. But to see him right then, he could have been a child being scolded for eating too many cookies. As sure as I knew my own name, I knew my brother-in-law was trying to find a way out of this mess, but it wasn't easy to come up with cause for him to be gallivanting around a human town with a vampire. Not while unexpectedly facing his father, who was angrier than a wet hen.

"He's here for me, sir," I said, my voice shaking on the words that weren't cracking. Add that to my trembling arms and chattering teeth, and I was a picture of masculine strength.

"He's here for what, now?" Mr. Smith asked incredulously.

"He's here for me, sir," I repeated, sounding just as terrified the second go-round. "I asked him to meet me so I could tell my sister how I've been. She worries about me, and you know she can't come into town none."

Where I'd come up with that line of bull, I couldn't rightly say, but it was out there now, and I reckoned it made enough sense to pass muster. Well, it would have made enough sense to pass muster if Mr. Smith had known thing one about me having mated a vampire or, at the very least, had an inkling that I'd moved off pack lands. Unfortunately, neither of those things was true.

"Why would Crissy need to come into town to talk to you?" Mr. Smith asked. "And why aren't you standing up like I said? We're going on home right now, and you can explain yourself on the way. Your father is going to be none too pleased when I tell him about this, boy."

Right. Well, I reckoned my parents weren't all that pleased about me having moved away. But I knew from Richie that Crissy had explained things to them, and though they didn't truly understand, they were relieved I was hale and healthy. Truly, we'd all thought I would pass before the year was through, and I reckon they figured having a living son was better than having a dead one, even if he was living off pack lands. With a vampire. All right, then, so not all shifters would think that was a fate better than death, but my folks were good, and my sister was a gem at explaining things and getting her way.

Be that as it may, I was now faced with a man who was much ornerier than my father, and I didn't have Crissy there to bridge the gap. I took a moment to think over my response, trying to choose words that would be least likely to infuriate the pack Beta, but in the end, I decided there was no way to sugarcoat the situation and I needed to just come out with it.

"I can't go with you, sir," I said. "My place is here now, with my mate." I gulped. "Richard Smith." I raised the hand that wasn't still clutching my vampire's shoulder and wished with all my might that it would stop its incessant shaking. "This here is Miguel Rodriguez." I pointed at Miguel. "My true mate."

Mr. Smith looked like he was fixin' to catch flies the way his mouth dropped and hung open.

"Shit," Richie said, finally speaking up. "Well, I reckon

you just told him how the cow ate the cabbage." He sighed deeply, looking like the weight of the world was on his shoulders. "Let's go, Papa."

"We ain't goin' nowhere without Ethan," Mr. Smith said through his clenched teeth. He'd gone from being unable to close his mouth to being unable to open it, all in the span of a few seconds. "Ethan Abbatt, you get yourself on up out of that there chair before I tear you out of it myself."

I still had my hand on Miguel's shoulder, and though I wouldn't have thought it possible, I could feel his muscles tightening further.

"I'm sorry, sir," I said. "But I ain't coming with you. I'm mated to Miguel, and a shifter's place is with his true mate."

Mr. Smith started to lean toward me, but Richie stopped him. "Papa," he said, his voice taking on an urgent note. "Ethan is right, and the humans are starting to stare. We need to leave."

The glare Richie received from his father would have taken a lesser man to his knees. "Ethan is right?" he asked incredulously. "He may be your wife's baby brother, Richie, but that no 'count runt ain't never been *right* for nothing but being put down and saving his kin some misery."

It seemed that there comment was the last straw as far as my mate was concerned, because he leaped to his feet and grabbed Mr. Smith by the shirt collar, somehow twisting the fabric so it cut into the man's neck. Then he lifted him up with just one arm until his toes barely touched the ground and leaned right into his face.

"Now you listen to me, you worthless piece of crap." Miguel's face was so full of rage that he was barely recognizable, and his voice teemed with danger. "You will never, and I do mean never, speak to Ethan that way again. Do I make myself clear?"

Oh, he was clear as day, no doubt about it. But seeing as how Mr. Smith's shirt was now acting as a noose, he was in no position to answer the question.

"Hey," Richie said as he started to reach for Miguel's arm. "Let go of my—"

Faster than my eyes could track, Miguel shot his free arm out and gripped Richie's throat, never once moving his eyes away from Mr. Smith.

"Do I make myself clear?" he asked again.

Mr. Smith nodded his now purple face, and Miguel released him, causing him to fall to his knees at our feet. He planted one hand on the floor to support himself and rubbed at his neck with the other as he coughed and gasped for air.

Still holding Richie's throat, Miguel leaned forward and whispered in his ear, "He's alive for one reason only—he's your father and Ethan seems to have an affinity for family. But you need to understand that that's a one-use-only pass. If he comes near Ethan again, relation or not, I will kill him." Miguel pushed Richie away and grinned down at his father, somehow finding a way to make that expression much more frightening than the scowl he'd worn prior. "And you better believe that I'll enjoy every last second of it."

All the blood seemed to drain from Richie's face, but

he still had the presence of mind to nod.

"I'm glad we understand each other," Miguel said, his voice as cold as ice. He turned around and cupped my nape with his big hand, then moved his thumb up and down the side of my neck in a soothing caress. I looked up and saw only warmth and affection aimed at me. "It's time to go, baby," he whispered.

I bobbed my head up and down and blinked rapidly, trying to process everything that had just taken place. It wasn't a surprise to hear that Mr. Smith thought ill of me. I'd always been different, always been weak. But never had the taunts thrown my way been quite that harsh. At least not right to my face.

And hearing a shifter bad-mouth a vampire, well, that wasn't new either. But somehow having that hatred directed at *my* vampire hurt in a way I hadn't expected.

"Well, ah..." I looked from Richie to his father and back again as I stood up. "I, uh..."

"Ethan?" Richie said. I flicked my gaze to his. "I'll make sure to let Crissy know you're well and that you're leavin' town."

His request came through loud and clear. Having me so close would be an ongoing source of conflict, which could only hurt my kin.

"Thank you, Richie," I said as I blinked back tears and leaned into Miguel's side. "I'm grateful."

I clutched Miguel's arm, needing his support, and he walked me past the nervous humans and out the door into the night.

CHAPTER 17

"TALK to me," Miguel said once we were back in his makeshift den.

I looked up at him and opened my mouth, but no words came out.

"Ethan, baby, you haven't said a word since we left that diner. You're starting to scare me now."

"I'm okay," I said, none too convincingly.

"You're shaking." He brushed my hair off my face and kissed my forehead. "How about we lie down? A lot's happened tonight, and I think some rest will do you good."

"Okay." I nodded and reached my trembling hand to my top shirt button. Unfortunately, I couldn't control my fingers enough to get a grip on the button.

"Here, let me do it," Miguel said. He moved my hand away and quickly had my white shirt unbuttoned, untucked, and on the ground. Then he divested me of my ragged jean shorts and sneakers and lowered me onto the mattress.

"Aren't you going to lie with me?" I asked when I saw that he was still fully dressed.

"Of course I am," he answered.

It didn't take but a few seconds for Miguel to strip out of

his black shirt and jeans and drop his briefs to the floor along with them. Then he kneeled down on the bed, unashamedly naked, and looked at me, his adoring gaze saying what he had yet to speak with words.

"I'm so sorry you had to experience that, Ethan. I know how much you care about your family."

My bottom lip trembled and I focused hard on holding back tears. "Richie doesn't think like his father, you know. And my folks, they ain't like that either. You've met Crissy so you've seen how wonderful she is, how much she loves me."

"Yes, I know, baby," he answered softly as he combed his fingers through my hair. He lay down on his side, propped himself up on his elbow, and continued to pet me gently. "But they didn't even tell the other shifters that you'd gone to be with me. You've told me that I'm your true mate and that shifters consider that rare and special—"

I turned my face and kissed his palm, the tightness in my chest loosening. "Yes," I mumbled against his skin. "I'm real blessed to have that, Miguel, to have you."

He sighed deeply. "Having me means they've essentially thrown you out of the pack," he said regretfully. "You do know that's what Richie was saying there at the end, right?"

"I do," I answered. "But if you feel regretful about that, Miguel, don't. I ain't never fit right in the pack. This isn't your fault." I moved my hand to his chest, skating it over smooth brown skin, enjoying the feeling of muscles rippling beneath the surface. "You're so beautiful," I whispered as I eased forward and kissed his nipple.

Miguel took my chin in his hand and tipped my face back so he could meet my gaze.

"Knowing what we do now, how they plan to treat you, we don't have to help them keep that land. They should be grateful we told them the land was being sold at all. Left on their own, they wouldn't have figured it out until it was too late because they think they're too good to talk to humans," he scoffed. "They can buy whatever they can afford and deal with humans owning the rest."

"No," I gasped. "Please, Miguel. We said we'd help them. We gave Richie and Crissy our word."

He looked taken aback. "Our word isn't binding. Even if I had some old-fashioned notion of honor—" He paused and looked in my eyes. "Which I don't, if the shifters won't let you onto pack lands, they've changed the rules of the agreement. They can't possibly expect us to buy land and let a bunch of shifters who won't let you onto that land use it at no charge."

"Sure they can," I said. "They're my pack, my family."

"After what they said tonight?" he asked disbelievingly. "Even though they've kicked you out?"

"Well, yeah," I said with a shrug. "That's the thing about family. You stand by each other through the hard times."

"They're not standing by you, Ethan." Miguel's voice took on that angry note.

I gave him a small smile. "No, they ain't," I said. "But if I took care of them only when they were being good to me, well, that'd be right simple. Standing by them when they're turning their backs on me..." I took a deep, calming breath, and then I looked into my mate's eyes. "Well, these are the hard times."

"They hurt you," Miguel said, sounding pained at the memory.

He was right, of course. The things Richie's father said had hurt. The fact that I was no longer welcome by my own pack hurt. The knowledge that I didn't know when or if I'd see my family again hurt. But I wasn't ready to think about those things yet.

"I burned my tongue," I said instead.

One side of Miguel's mouth turned up in a grin. "You burned your tongue?"

"Uh-huh. I drank that coffee a mite too quick and got scalded."

Miguel cupped my cheek and ran his thumb over my jaw. "Let me see," he said.

I parted my lips and stuck my tongue out.

"Oh, I see," he said. "How about I kiss it and make it better?"

I whimpered, and he smiled tenderly as he flipped his leg over my hip so he was straddling me. He cupped my cheeks and then dipped down, covering our faces in a veil of silky black hair. Then he started lapping at my tongue. Surprisingly enough, his licks seemed to make the burn less painful, like when he sealed the wounds made by his fangs. Those licks also made my shaft grow longer.

"Miguel," I moaned.

He sucked my tongue into his mouth and moved his

hands up my temples until he had tangled his fingers in my hair. I arched up as I dug my fingers into his back. When he finally pulled away, his eyes were full of heat, full of lust, and all for me.

"I want you," I said.

He propped his forearms on either side of me and then straightened his body in a way that slid his skin against mine.

"Oh!" I cried out when his thick, hard shaft brushed alongside mine.

"I want you too," he whispered huskily into my ear and rocked on top of me, giving us both the friction we craved.

I spread my legs wide and canted my hips up, causing his hot steel to press against my pecker, my testicles, and even the area beneath. It felt so good I nearly lost my breath.

"Ungh," I moaned and tipped my head back, exposing the throbbing veins in my neck to my vampire.

He shot forward and pressed his lips to my exposed skin, sucking hard enough to leave yet another mark on my body. With me wiggling beneath him and his erection rubbing against me, I started to crave something we hadn't yet tried.

"Miguel," I said.

"Yes," he answered.

"I want you to... Do you want to..."

"Oh, yeah," he groaned and slid his hand between my legs, rubbing his fingers up and down my crease. "I want to."

I couldn't respond with words, just a sound that was part moan, part whimper, and all need. Miguel kissed and bit and sucked his way down my body, pinching skin his mouth couldn't reach with one hand while the other maintained its place in my nether regions, rubbing, exploring, and every so often penetrating my hole with thick fingers. By the time he reached my groin with his mouth, I was shaking and panting, an almost constant stream of cries and moans pouring from my mouth.

"Look at you," he said reverently from his perch between my thighs. I looked down to see him staring at the dark purple head of my swollen shaft. "Dripping for me." He flicked his tongue out and licked up the moisture seeping from my crown. "Taste so damn good," he whispered, turning me on even more. "Bet you taste delicious all over."

He dragged his tongue down my prick and over my testicles. Then he pushed my knees up until my feet were planted on the bed, cupped the globes of my backside in his large hands, and spread me apart, exposing my hidden area to him. When he dipped his face down and started licking and nibbling at the sensitive skin there, I went wild, crying out his name, grasping at the sheets, and gasping for air.

"Oh, yeah," Miguel said with a deep chuckle. "I was right. You are delicious everywhere."

The words stopped after that because his mouth was too busy driving me out of my ever-loving mind. The licking and sucking didn't stop, but it did get progressively more concentrated in a certain area until, finally, I felt my mate's tongue pushing at my hole.

"Ah!" I shouted when that wet muscle entered my body, moving in and out and side to side. I grabbed for his hair, holding him in place as I pushed down and circled my hips against his face. "Yes! Oh, Lord, feels good. So good, Miguel."

I didn't know how long my mate stayed in that position, laving my hole and playing my body like a fiddle, but by the time he pulled his lips back and pressed his fingers in, I was dripping with his saliva and desperate to be filled.

He got to his knees and lifted my legs onto his thighs, spreading me open. "I'm going in now," he said as he placed the head of his shaft against my hole.

"Please," I answered.

Not wasting a second, he rocked forward and penetrated my body in a new way. He didn't stop until his testicles were squished against me. Then he lay on me, wiggled his arms under my back, and held onto my shoulders, keeping me still as he dragged his shaft out and then shoved it back in.

I wrapped my legs around him, resting my heels on his backside, and clung to his arms as I met each and every one of his powerful thrusts. We grunted and moaned, our lips meeting for kiss after kiss as Miguel impaled me over and over again. With his stomach pressing and rubbing against my hard length and his erection dragging against that wonderful spot inside me, I fell into a sea of pleasure.

"Miguel, ungh, I'm going to... Miguel!"

Hot white seed shot from my shaft and left a slick path between us. Miguel roared and rose to his knees. He pushed my thighs up and spread them out, then he started jackhammering into me—hard, fast, and relentless. Soon he tipped his head back, stretched his neck, clenched his jaw, and ground against me as he shouted my name and pulsed his life essence into me.

When his body had released all its seed, he dropped on top of me and nuzzled my throat. I tilted my chin up in invitation, and Miguel accepted my offer, sinking his fangs into my vein and taking long, slow pulls. We lay together, him drinking, me petting his hair, and I realized that despite what had happened at the diner earlier that night, I was happy. Really and truly happy, deep down. And it was because of the man who was, at that moment lapping at my neck.

He flipped onto his back and pulled me on top of him, yanked the blanket over us, and then held me tight, so tight.

"Are you doing okay, baby?" he asked, sounding warm and relaxed.

"I am," I answered, knowing that though I'd lost a lot that day, I'd gained much more. "I'm great."

"Where're you going?" I asked when I felt the bed shift as my mate climbed out. My tongue felt thick in my mouth, my words came out slow, and it was all I could do to open my eyes. I was exhausted.

"Shhh, you sleep." Miguel petted my hair. "I'm going to go get you some food."

I draped my arm around his waist and laid my head on his thigh. "'M not hungry," I mumbled.

"You will be when you wake up. There's a few hours

yet till sunrise. I'll go get you something to eat."

I rubbed my eyes and started sitting up. "I'll go with you," I said.

Miguel put his hand on my back and kept me in place. "No. Tomorrow's a big day. We're leaving Kfarkattan at sunset. You need all the rest you can get."

"We're leaving?" I looked up at Miguel's handsome face. "So soon?"

He traced my eyebrow with his finger. "It's time, wolf. Now that Richie's father knows where you are, after what happened with him, you're not safe here." He moved his hand to my nape and massaged me. "Besides, there's nothing left for us to do. We bought the land like we promised. I'll get word to the humans that we want to expand the plot size." He grinned at me. "And now we need to go home."

"Home," I repeated.

"Yes. One of my houses is near a lake. It's warm there this time of year, and we can swim at night. Would you like that?"

I scrunched my eyebrows together. "I ain't ever been swimming, but I've always wanted to try. I like the water."

Miguel's expression lightened and he beamed at me, all the while continuing to run his fingers through my hair. "Good. Then it's settled. We'll go there and see if you like it. There's a really nice caretaker's cottage at the edge of the cemetery. It has plenty of space and all the modern amenities."

"How will we get there?" I asked.

"We'll drive."

"You have a car?"

Miguel nodded. "I do. It'll take a few days, so we'll need to make some stops along the way when the sun's out, but I know of some good inns, so that won't be a problem."

"That sounds nice," I said softly, the gentle strokes of my mate's hand lulling me back to sleep.

"What's that?" he asked.

"Going on a car trip with you. Holing up in fancy hotels during the day. Living in a house by a lake, just the two of us." I sighed wistfully and closed my eyes. "Sounds nice."

I felt Miguel get up, but I was too tired to protest again, so I just fell back to sleep, hoping he'd be back by the time I woke.

CHAPTER 18

"Well, you're pretty. I'll give him that much."

I shot up in bed and scrambled as far as I could from the stranger sneering down at me. Well, he wasn't really a stranger. I mean, he'd torn into me, pinned me to a wall, and watched me nearly bleed out as he tried to kill me. I supposed that meant we were somewhat acquainted.

"What are you doing here?" I asked Ralph as I grappled for the blanket and pulled it up to my chin.

"I think the more interesting question," he said as he stepped closer, "is what you're doing here, dog."

I was in the corner of the room, an angry vampire between me and the door. Things could have been better.

"This here is Miguel's room," I answered.

"Yes." Ralph put one foot on the mattress. He was fully dressed, shoes included. That there was just poor manners. "It is Miguel's room." His second foot joined the first. I hoped he hadn't stepped in any mud. "And yet you're here. In his bed." He shoved his foot under the blanket, kicked it up, caught it with his hand, and then yanked it off me. "Naked."

I pulled my knees up to my chest and wrapped my arms around them, shielding as much of myself as I could from his prying gaze.

"Well?" he said.

Was he expecting me to say something? Because I hadn't heard a question in there. It seemed he had summed things up quite nicely. Plus, anything I could have said was right likely to antagonize him further. I was young, not stupid, so I kept my mouth shut. Seemed to me from the little bit I knew about this particular vampire, that there was a lesson he could have taken to heart.

I heard a door open and somebody running down the stairs. I already recognized Miguel's gait, both by sight and sound, so I knew it wasn't him. I must have been really out of it to have slept through Ralph's descent into the basement. Miguel had been right to tell me I needed sleep.

"Ralph?" That was Ted's voice. "Hector said you were down here."

I was guessing Hector was one of their vampire friends. I'd never received formal introductions.

"In here," Ralph shouted over his shoulder.

Ted came running in and stumbled to a stop just inside the doorway. "What's going on?" he said, looking back and forth between me, cowering naked in the corner, and Ralph, towering over me and tracking who knew what onto the mattress.

"I was just asking Miguel's dog here the very same thing," he said as he gestured to me with his chin.

It wasn't technically a true statement. I mean, he'd said a few things, sure enough, but he hadn't asked any questions.

I reckoned correcting him would just rile him further, and seeing as how he seemed more than a bit off-kilter, I decided against it.

"Shit!" Ted said. "We have just enough time to find shelter nearby before the sun rises, but we can't lose any more time." He sounded downright panicked. "Come on, we need to leave now."

Ralph crossed his arms over his chest. "Now why would we do that? I just got here and I'm in no rush to leave."

"Are you kidding me?" Ted asked disbelievingly. He looked at Ralph like the man was just eat up with stupid. Which, bless his heart, seemed to be an ongoing problem. "When Miguel finds you here, he *will* kill you."

"Well, then, it's a good thing he's not going to find me, now isn't it?" Ralph said darkly.

Ted's jaw dropped. "What have you done?" he asked in a near whisper, fear laced through every word.

"I took care of our problem." Ralph shrugged his shoulders and smirked at Ted, who seemed to be finding no humor in the situation.

"Our problem?" Ted repeated. "What problem?"

"What problem," Ralph scoffed. "Your bossy unbalanced friend, that's what problem."

"Oh, fuck." Ted's face paled before my eyes, which was quite a feat because the man wasn't exactly sporting a tan under the best of circumstances. "What have you done?"

"I just told you, I took—"

Ted moved forward and grasped Ralph's upper arms,

shaking him hard. I rather hoped it would bring the man to his senses, but to that point I'd seen neither hide nor hair of any sense nearby. "This isn't a joke!" Ted shouted. "Do you have any idea who you're messing with? Miguel Rodriguez is—"

"You have a thing for him, I get it!" Ralph said as he planted his hands on Ted's chest and shoved him back. "But he's gone, so you're going to have deal with it and move on."

"What, are you jealous?" Ted said, sounding truly surprised.

I didn't know why. I was on Ralph's side on this one; to my mind, Ted seemed a fair bit too infatuated with *my* mate. I would have said so and let him know he didn't stand a chance, but my good buddy Ralph seemed to have things under control. That, and I reckoned he'd kill me if I so much as opened my mouth and reminded him that I was still in the room.

Ralph snorted. "Oh, please. Why would I be jealous?"

There were lots of reasons, actually, but it didn't seem the time or place to get into them. Besides, trying to explain something to Ralph was as useless as tits on a bull.

"I don't know, and you know what? I don't care. At this point I'm just trying to keep you alive long enough to see another sunset. It's too late for us to go anywhere, but I can probably talk Miguel into letting us stay in one of the rooms upstairs just for today. I know he said you couldn't come back here, but maybe if I—"

"He's gone!" Ralph shouted furiously. "Why aren't you

listening to me? I got rid of him, so it doesn't matter what he said. We can stay here as long as we want. I can stay here as long as I want."

All right, now I had to admit I was getting a tad nervous. Not much, mind you, because I was certain I'd be able to feel it in my soul if my mate was gone, so I knew Ralph was mistaken. Still, hearing that sunrise was so near and not seeing Miguel in the room, well, it was cause for some concern. All in all, I decided that a bit of worry was a good thing because it distracted me just enough to keep me from laughing at the vampire in front of me, who seemed to be doing an impression of a toddler throwing a fit.

"What exactly do you mean, you got rid of him? You can't get rid of Miguel. He's four centuries old, did you know that?"

Not having any idea about the age of other vampires, I didn't realize Miguel's age was unusual. It must have been at least a bit out of the ordinary, though, because for the first time since he walked into the room, something other than haughty confidence crossed over Ralph's face.

True to form, the vampire shook off any indication of common sense right quick. "Well, as soon as the sun rises, those centuries are coming to a close."

"And why is that?" Ted asked, his voice taking on a high-pitched quality. "What'd you do, Ralph?"

The vampire shrugged. "We all came down here to buy land, and your buddy thinks he can just sweep in and take it all out from under us. He had no right to do that. I decided he needed to be taught a lesson."

"You—" Ted gulped. "You and your three friends together barely have enough money to buy a tiny plot of land and you decided to teach him a lesson?"

"Well, you have enough, and you were going to let me stay with you, right? But then he ruined it all, so we tied him up outside." Ralph looked very pleased with himself. "See? I told you I got rid of him."

"You tied him up and you think it'll hold him?" Ted asked. "Don't you remember how he got out of the chains you used last time? You think he was mad then? When he gets out of the restraints this time, he'll—"

"He's not getting out of them this time! We used twice as many chains."

"We?"

"Yeah. Me and Pedro and Anthony and Andre. Your friend Hector is a pussy, but we didn't need him anyway. Because after I heard Miguel bought up all that land, I called in reinforcements. They're all watching him now. Eight vampires. He's hanging out a window and the chains are long enough to reach inside where they can hold onto them. So you see? I have it all handled. He's not getting out of it this time. Just as soon as the sun rises, Miguel Rodriguez will burn."

It all sounded pretty ominous, and I'll confess that my heart might have sped up just a hair, but I had seen my mate's strength firsthand, and I had faith that he'd come back to me. Ted, on the other hand, looked like he was about to have a heart attack. Well, that was, if vampires could have heart attacks, which I was fairly sure they couldn't.

"It's going to be a bloodbath," Ted said under his breath in horror. He glared at Ralph. "What building? Where are they?"

"Why do you want to know? You won't get there in time to save him."

"I'm not trying to save him!" Ted shouted. "He's strong enough to save himself." It was comforting to hear Ted speak aloud what I knew deep in my soul. "I'm trying to save your idiot friends from him. You weren't turned long ago, so you don't understand how rare it is for a vampire to survive as long as he has. It doesn't happen by accident. Miguel is strong, even more so now than he's been in all the years I've known him. This plan you've hatched is going to backfire and—"

"It's too late anyway," Ralph said. "The sun is rising."

Almost as if on cue, footsteps and shouting rent the air. We all turned toward the door to see two vampires dragging themselves in. Their clothes were hanging in shreds and soaked in blood, their exposed skin was covered in abrasions, and their expressions showed pure, unadulterated terror. It was like something out of a ghost story we used to tell each other as kids. I had to turn my head from the sight before I emptied the contents of my stomach on the bed. That would have been worse than the dirty shoes.

"What's going on?" Ralph shouted.

One of the vampires, whom I was fairly sure I recognized from the warehouse interactions, though it was hard to tell with his face coated in blood and dirt and scratches, opened his mouth to answer, but instead, blood gurgled out and he clutched his own throat and collapsed. Ted immediately dropped to his knees and pressed his hands onto the largest gashes, trying to curb the bleeding.

Ralph turned to the other vampire. "Pedro?" he squeaked out, his voice quivering.

"They're gone," Pedro said.

"Who?"

"All of them." Pedro's eyes were wide. "He was killing all of them." He shook his head as if hoping to shove out the memory. "I've never seen anything like it." He gulped. "He... he somehow climbed up the chains and into the window. They were around his throat, he should have choked, but he didn't. He just kept screaming something about his mate; it didn't make sense." He dragged his trembling fingers through his hair. "And then he got in and we tried to run, but he was too fast and there was screaming, so much screaming, and blood." He paused for a few moments and gasped for air. "He pulled their hearts out of their chests with his bare hands, tore their heads off. Anthony and I were closest to the door, so we were able to get away."

He looked up at Ralph, his face anguished. "Why?" His voice broke on the word. "Why did we have to do that? He'd been letting us stay with him, teaching us things. Everything was fine until you started fighting with him. And Hector told you it was a bad idea! He *told* you. But you wouldn't listen and now..." Pedro's legs seemed to give out from under him, and he curled up on the floor, shaking and crying.

I don't know how I expected Ralph to react to that horrifying scene, but it certainly wasn't to have him turn his angry, hate-filled eyes on me.

"He thinks he can kill my friends?" he asked, though I could only assume it was rhetorical because Pedro had just explained to us in graphic detail that not only did Miguel *think* he could kill Ralph's friends, but he had in fact done so. "Well, let's see how he feels about me killing his new little pet."

"Ralph." Ted sounded tired. He was still crouching on the ground over an unconscious Anthony, and I noticed that he'd peeled off his own shirt and torn it into strips of fabric that he was now tying around Anthony's wounds. "For your own sake, stop." He looked up at Ralph. "Leave. Run as far as you can and hope he won't bother looking for you."

Ralph was now within arm's distance of me, and there was no way for me to curl myself into a smaller ball. He looked at Ted over his shoulder. "You'll come with me?" he asked.

"No." Ted shook his head. "I'm not leaving Miguel."

"You don't think he'll kill you too?" Ralph asked. "You brought me along." He waved his hand toward the door. "You brought all of us along. He'll blame you for what happened just as much as he'll blame me, and then you'll end up like them." He cocked his chin toward Pedro and Anthony's bodies.

"If he does, then he does," Ted said. "I'll take what's coming to me for my part in all of this." He tore another strip from his shirt and wrapped it around yet another bleeding gash on the other vampire. "Miguel turned me. I won't leave him."

"But you'll leave me? You turned me."

"I did," Ted said, not raising his gaze from his task of tending to the wounds. "And it was a mistake."

Ted was looking down at the injured vampires, doing what he could to save them, so he couldn't see the rage that crossed Ralph's face, couldn't see him flip around so he now faced Ted, couldn't see him leap forward, aiming at Ted with murder in his eyes.

But I was off to the side, so I could see it all. And though I'd been jealous of Ted's history with my mate, something that wasn't at all alleviated by the new knowledge that Miguel had turned him and that Ted was willing to stand by his side even at the risk of his own death, I found myself admiring this particular vampire. His feelings ran deep, I could tell. He'd cared for the injured vampires at his own peril. He was loyal to my mate. In a roundabout way, I reckoned that made him a friend, even if he didn't know it. And I didn't exactly have a swarm of friends buzzing around.

"No!" I shouted as I jumped out of my crouch and stole Ralph's attention back to me. "Don't!"

CHAPTER 19

AT THE sound of my voice, Ted jerked his head up and seemed to realize that Ralph was either aiming at him or at the wounded vampires he was tending. He gathered the men together as tight as he could and covered their bodies with his own in a defensive posture.

Thankfully, Ralph was no longer focusing on Ted, but instead was back to sneering at me. The way the man's head kept turning from one of us to the other made it seem as if we were playing a to-the-death version of Ping-Pong. Not nearly as safe, but endlessly more entertaining.

"So the dog finally speaks," he said to me, staying consistent with the line of insults he'd started the moment we met. Well, he meant them to be insulting, but, honestly, I liked dogs. They were smart, loyal, and brave, and, frankly, I could do much worse than to be compared to those particular animals.

"Let's see how well Miguel trained his little pet." Ralph stepped toward me, and because we were standing on the mattress, we both jiggled a tad. "Sit," he said, pointing at his feet.

I didn't move. Well, I didn't move into a sitting position.

I did move, though, because he was walking, which caused the mattress to bounce all over.

"No? Tsk, tsk, tsk. Looks like the illustrious Miguel Rodriguez isn't a very good pet owner. Okay, how about this one?" He took another step toward me and almost lost his balance so he had to throw his arms out to his sides. "Beg," he said.

His steps were harder now. I flattened my palm on the wall so I wouldn't fall over.

"Can't get that one right either?" He shook his head disapprovingly. "Looks like I won't be able to keep you, pet. Nobody wants a dog who can't follow basic commands. I'll give you one last chance." He squinted and curled his lips just enough for his fangs to point out, then he lifted his hand in the air and showed me his claws. "Die."

Having already felt those particular sharp points digging into my flesh during our first meeting, I wasn't keen to repeat the experience, so I ducked and jumped under his flailing arm.

He did a slow turn and patted his knee. "Here, puppy, puppy, puppy. Here, puppy."

I didn't know whether he was aiming for insane or terrifying, but either way his goal was thwarted because I jumped out of reach, which made the springs contract and release in short order and took his feet out from under him.

"Argh!" he shouted in frustration and tried to rise up on his feet.

I say "tried" because I kept running in circles, so the

mattress kept bouncing and he couldn't stay steady enough to hold his balance. Eventually, he put his hands on the mattress and pushed himself up onto all fours before slowly straightening his legs and then standing up. I hadn't forgotten that I was dealing with a bloodthirsty vampire, but, truly, in that moment, he more closely resembled an uncoordinated toddler.

While Ralph and I had been doing our little dance of imminent death, or humiliating sprawl, depending on your perspective, Ted seemed to have taken advantage of the distraction and dragged Anthony out the door and then returned to do the same with Pedro. There was no way for me to escape from the room short of shoving them out of the way, which I wouldn't do, even if I'd been strong enough.

I plastered myself to the wall and tried to inch away from the angry vampire stalking me. He threw his head back and cackled, which, let's face it, was pretty ridiculous. I mean, the man was a vampire, not a witch in a children's tale. Anyway, he cackled and raised his clawed hand in the air, ready to eviscerate me, when his gaze zeroed in on my neck.

He froze.

"Are those..." He squinted and stepped closer. "They are," he said. "Those are teeth marks." He snapped his head up and looked at me in surprise. "He's been feeding from you."

"What?" Ted was halfway out the door, but he stopped and looked back at us when he heard Ralph's accusation.

Ralph darted his gaze all over my body and furrowed his brow. "I thought we couldn't do that. You're a shifter." He tipped his head forward and sniffed a few times. "Yeah, I can smell it. You're carrying Miguel's scent, but there's that rotten shifter scent there too. So how is it that he can feed from you?"

Like the other questions the vampire had thrown my way, I didn't reckon that one required a response. Besides, I didn't have one, or at least not one he'd have been able to understand. I somehow doubted we had enough time before the imminently scheduled killing to discuss true mates and the fact that I wasn't so much carrying Miguel's scent as it was now braided with mine.

"It's all a lie, isn't it?" he said excitedly, sounding like he'd solved some great mystery. "I bet shifters aren't poisonous at all. He made it all up to keep the rest of us on human blood so he could have the shifter blood to himself, didn't he?"

Honestly, there was a tree stump in a Louisiana swamp with a higher IQ.

"Why would Miguel do that, Ralph?" Ted snapped. "Listen to yourself! You're not making any sense."

Ted was right. Ralph wasn't making sense. I mean, sure Miguel had told me he'd felt stronger, warmer, better after drinking from me, but that was because we were true mates. I knew it. And, besides, I'd heard many a tale of pack members who'd been in fights with vampires and gotten out alive only because the vampires ingested their blood and died. The idea that one lone vampire could perpetuate a lie that big and get away with it only made sense in Ralph's miniature world of logic.

Unfortunately for Ralph, and fortunately for me, Ted's accusation seemed to inflame Ralph further rather than calm him down.

"Oh yeah?" he said. "I'll prove it to you." He jumped forward and pinned me to the wall. I tried to wiggle free, but he shoved his knee into my groin and clasped my hands in his. "Quit moving!" he shouted as he tried to wedge my head back and get at my throat.

"What are you doing?" Ted asked. "Are you... You're not going to feed from him, are you?" Ralph couldn't answer because he was too busy wrestling with me. "You know what?" Ted finally said in frustration. "Go ahead." He let go of Pedro's still unconscious body, crossed his arms over his chest, and stared at us.

I was surprised enough by that permission to snap my focus to Ted, which moved my attention away from Ralph for just a second. That was all he needed to strike. He rushed forward and clamped his jaw on my neck, breaking the skin with his fangs and releasing a current of blood into his mouth.

That felt nothing like Miguel's bite. It made my skin crawl and it hurt like all get-out. I was ready to kick and claw my way out of that mess, but then Ralph pulled his head back and looked at me wide-eyed before he started convulsing madly. He collapsed to the floor within seconds, shaking and wetting himself, and then he let out a final, pained wail and went limp.

I pressed my hand up against my bleeding neck and applied pressure, trying to speed up my already fast clotting process. A few seconds ticked by and Ralph didn't move so much as an inch, so I reached my foot out and poked his body. He didn't budge, just lay there in his own filth. Well, his own and that of the other two vampires who'd bled all over the floor. Dirt on the mattress or no, I wasn't sleeping in that room ever again.

"Well, there you have it," Ted said. I tore my gaze over to him. "Seems he proved a point after all." He shook his head. "Some people really are too stupid to live."

We stood in silence for a few minutes, both of us looking at Ralph's body. Then Ted sighed, heaved Pedro back into his arms, and continued dragging him out of the room, and I moved my hand from my no-longer-bleeding neck.

"Need some help?" I asked.

"Yeah," he grunted. "That'd be great. He's heavy as hell, and after carrying Anthony out of here, I'm worn out."

Ted had his arms curled under Pedro's armpits and he was supporting Pedro's back on his chest. I stepped between the vampire's legs, squatted down, and put his knees over my elbows before standing back up.

"You got him?" Ted asked.

I nodded and we slowly made our way out of the room.

"Where are we taking him?" I asked.

"Uh, so far my plan was just to get as far away as possible from Miguel's sleeping quarters so he doesn't finish what he started with these two when he comes back."

I growled deep in my chest and bared my teeth at the vampire. "Miguel didn't start nothing!" I barked. "He was defending himself."

Ted jerked his head up and looked taken aback by my reaction. Fair enough. I supposed I hadn't been all that angry about Ralph's shenanigans, but then again, he hadn't been insulting my mate. To his credit, though, Ted recovered quickly. "I'm sorry," he said. "That was a poor choice of words. I didn't mean it like that. I just meant that they attacked him and got away. That's not the kind of thing Miguel is going to let pass easily, and finding them in his space is just going to make it worse."

I grunted as an acceptance of his apology, and we kept walking until we reached the stairs. Anthony was sitting on the ground, leaning against the wall next to the staircase and dragging what looked to be painful breaths into his lungs. We propped Pedro up next to him.

"Are they going to be okay?" I asked.

"I don't know," Ted said. "I did the best I could for them, but I'm not a healer."

"Well, then it's a good thing I'm here," a female voice said from the top of the staircase.

Ted and I both jerked our heads up. "Katherine?" he said. "Is that you?"

"Get out of my way, Katie, or you're going to need a healer yourself." Oh, Lord, Miguel. The sound of my mate's voice made my knees go weak. His rapid footsteps sounded on the stairs. "Ethan!" he shouted. "Ethan!"

"I'm here." My voice cracked, so I cleared my throat and tried again. "I'm here!"

Moments later I was swept into strong arms and cradled against a broad chest. I clung to Miguel's shirt and buried my face against his shoulder. He cupped the back of my head with one big hand and palmed my lower back with the other.

"Where's Ralph?" he asked as he darted his gaze around the room.

"Dead," I told him.

He sighed in relief and some of the tension left his body. "Good," he said. "He didn't hurt you, did he? Tell me you're okay."

"Miguel," Ted said as he stepped toward us. "Nothing—"

"Don't!" Miguel growled and turned around, shielding me from the other vampire's view. It didn't make much sense because Ted and I had been alone together just moments prior, but I wasn't going to argue. I was much too busy climbing my mate like a tree. "You're lucky to be breathing after bringing that fucking waste of air into our lives," Miguel said to Ted. I wrapped my legs around his waist, which seemed to distract him because he stopped yelling and moved his hand down to cup my backside.

"Ted," the female said, garnering my attention just long enough for me to identify her by scent as a vampire. "Be grateful that little wolf is here, because he's the only reason Miguel hasn't taken your head off. Your friends here don't seem to have been as lucky, so get over here and help me try to save them."

Figuring they had the situation under control and we were out of danger, I nuzzled and licked at Miguel's neck. "So glad you're here," I said, my voice shaky.

"Shhh. It's all okay now." Miguel peppered kisses along my jawline and over to my ear. "You didn't have to worry. I promised I wouldn't leave you, and a certain someone taught me that it was very important to keep my word."

I laughed around the tears now welling up in my eyes. "I know." I sniffled. "I knew you'd be back. I did. Ralph said..." I gulped. "Well, he said he'd killed you, but I wasn't worried none because I knew it weren't true."

Miguel tangled his fingers in my hair and tugged just enough to make me raise my face and look into his eyes. His hair was a bit matted, some blood streaked his cheek, dirt was smeared across his forehead, and he looked even more beautiful than I remembered.

"You knew it wasn't true, did you?" He grinned at me. "And just how did you know that?"

"Because I'd have felt it if you'd passed." I met his gaze. "We're connected at the soul, remember?"

He swallowed loudly. "I do," he said. "Now, do you care to tell me why I walked in here and found you naked with another man?" He raised one eyebrow and looked at me expectantly.

"Oh, for crying out loud!" I said in amusement. "Don't you choose this here moment to start getting jealous, now. I didn't have time to get my clothes on because I was running for my life on your unusually bouncy mattress." Seriously. Where had he gotten that thing?

Miguel's expression darkened right quick and he furrowed his brow. "Running for your life?" He held me tighter and slowly panned around to look at Ted. "Who exactly was threatening your life?"

Ted must have heard our conversation because, though he'd been helping the female vampire, Katherine, tend to Pedro, his hands quickly flew in the air in a defensive posture and his face flushed.

"Ralph," I said quickly, not wanting Miguel to confuse my new sort-of-friend as my attacker. "It was just Ralph."

I heard a rumbling deep in his chest and his nostrils flared. "And he's dead?" he asked.

"Yes," I assured him.

"Where's his body?"

"Uh." I gulped. "It's by our bed."

Miguel marched straight back to our room. I dropped my forehead down onto his wide shoulder and squeezed my eyes shut, not wanting to see the destruction again. Even without my vision, I knew the second we stepped into that room. The stench of urine and blood was overpowering.

A grunt of approval from Miguel told me he'd seen Ralph's body. "Who killed him?" he asked. Suddenly, Miguel pushed my head back and started sniffing at my neck. I reckoned he'd finally calmed down enough about my well-being to start registering more details about his surroundings.

He was not going to be happy about the destruction of his extra-bouncy mattress. "He bit you!" he roared.

His body jerked and then I heard a loud thump. It took me a moment to realize Miguel had kicked Ralph's body across the room.

"I'm okay," I said soothingly. "He didn't hurt me none."

"He bit you," Miguel said again, sounding pained, and then he started sniffing at the spot on my neck where Ralph had violated me with his fangs.

"Yes, he did," I admitted. "But, hey, I had the last laugh, right?" I chuckled uncomfortably. "I mean, it was his last bite. Ever." Even as I said it, I felt sick at the realization. I'd killed a man.

"Ethan?" Miguel said. "You're trembling. Why are you trembling?"

"I...I killed him. I didn't mean to do it and he was trying to hurt me, but still. I killed him."

"Oh, baby." Miguel sighed. "Let me get our things and get you out of here. I think we could both use a bath."

I tightened my legs around his waist and fisted his shirt in both hands. "Don't you let me go," I begged. "Please."

Thankfully, he gave heed to my words. He walked around the room, gathering our belongings and stuffing them into both our bags with one hand while he continued to hang onto me with the other. Because neither of us had much, it didn't take long before Miguel draped a long shirt over my nude body and we left the room.

Ted and Katherine were still next to the stairs, caring

for Pedro and Anthony, both of whom were now awake and looking like they might survive. They cringed and whimpered when they caught sight of Miguel approaching them.

"He won't hurt you," Katherine said. "Relax."

"I already hurt them," Miguel reminded the vampires. "And I might do it again. More thoroughly. Like I did to their dead friends. I haven't decided."

Katherine glared up at my mate. "Miguel!" she shouted. "Don't tease them. They're in no condition for your humor."

Miguel flashed his fangs at her. "I'm not teasing, Katie, and I could give a fuck about their condition. They tried to keep me away from my mate!"

I gasped. It was the first time he'd acknowledged the nature of our connection out loud, and the joy it brought nearly took my breath away. It also made my pecker stand up and take notice, which was a miracle considering the current situation.

"Miguel," I whispered. "Can we have that bath now?"

"Sure we can, baby," he said tenderly. "Ted," he snapped.

"Yes." Ted's anxiety was apparent from just that word.

"You brought the trash in here and you'll see to it that it's cleared out of my room, won't you?"

"I will," Ted answered, and then he sighed in relief at what I reckoned was Miguel's display of forgiveness for his part in that day's fiasco. "Thank you."

CHAPTER 20

THERE was a room in the warehouse that had running water and a bathtub. Miguel had boarded up the window, just as he had throughout the rest of the warehouse, so we'd had the pleasure of bathing during the night and the day. He climbed the basement steps with me in his arms and walked us over to the bathroom.

"Are you okay to stand?" he asked, not making a move to set me onto my feet until I nodded. Even then he lowered me slowly, gently, and made sure I was steady before pulling his hand away. The shirt he'd draped over me fell to the floor.

"I'm fine," I said with a laugh. "Honest. I wasn't hurt." I shrugged. "I just wanted to be close to you." I rubbed my toe on the floor. "I guess maybe I was a tad more frightened than I realized."

He flung his arm around my waist and pulled me into a hug. "I'm so sorry, baby," he said. "I didn't mean to bring all this down on you."

"None of this was your fault," I said. "If anything, it was my fault. To hear Ralph tell it, he was mad about your decision to buy up the pack lands."

"Ralph was a fool who deserved what he got," Miguel

said angrily. He pressed his fingers to the spot on my neck where Ralph had bitten me. "He had no right to touch you, to bite you."

I put my hand over Miguel's. "He's dead," I reminded him.

"I know. I wish I could bring him back to life just so I could kill him all over again."

I couldn't help but laugh at that comment.

Miguel arched one eyebrow. "You think that's funny, do you?"

"No." I shook my head and chuckled some more. "It's really not."

"And yet you're laughing."

"Yeah." I beamed at him. "Thanks for that."

He smiled back at me, and we stood there for a few moments, staring at each other and grinning like a couple of loons.

"All right," Miguel said eventually. "Bath time." He squatted down and turned on the tap that came out of the wall on the side of the tub. He put his hand underneath the stream to check the temperature before standing back up. "Climb on in," he said.

I did as he said and settled down on the hard surface, then immediately reached for the soap and began scrubbing myself clean.

Miguel toed off his shoes and then hooked his thumbs in the sides of his pants and pushed them down, exposing his torn-up legs.

I gasped in horror and dropped the soap. "Oh my Lord!" I shouted and reached for him.

"I'm fine," he said. "Just a few scratches, and they're already scabbing over."

When he peeled his shirt off, I almost passed out. There didn't seem to be a single bit of skin that wasn't covered in deep, angry gashes. Those black clothes he favored must have hidden a lot of blood because my mate was much more hurt than I'd realized.

He climbed into the tub and the water immediately turned pink. I reached a trembling hand for the soap I'd dropped and hesitated.

"Will it hurt too much for me to wash you?" I asked.

"Nothing could ever hurt enough to make me turn down your touch," he said.

Taking him at his word, I lathered up my hands and carefully ran them over his body and head, alternating handfuls of water with soap until his hair was silky and smooth and the water around us ran clear.

"The water's still warm," Miguel said. "I can plug the drain and fill the tub if you want to sit here for a bit."

"That'd be right nice," I told him.

Once he had the plug in the drain, he relaxed back against the tub, spread his legs wide, and held his arms open. "C'mere," he said.

I turned around and scooted until my back was pressed against his chest.

"This doesn't hurt you, does it?" I asked.

He wrapped his arms around my chest and pulled me tighter.

"Uh-uh," he said and nuzzled my neck. Then he stiffened and I could hear a rumble in his broad chest. "I can smell him on you." Anger laced his words.

"I washed real good," I told him.

"Doesn't matter. He's still there, under the skin."

My heart raced and my breathing quickened. I didn't want anyone but my mate under my skin. "Get him out, Miguel." I dropped my head back on his shoulder and rested my arms over his. "I need you."

He moved his big hands down my chest, over my belly, across my groin, and over to my thighs. "You're not hurt, right?"

I dropped my knees to the sides and canted my hips up, giving him better access. "Not hurt. Promise," I whispered.

He cupped my testicles with one hand and wrapped the other around my hard length. Then he fondled and stroked me as he licked and sucked at my neck, pulling the blood close to the surface.

"Ungh," I moaned and thrust up into his fist. He scraped his fangs against my neck and tightened his hand around my testicles. "Please," I cried.

His response was immediate. Sharp teeth sank into my skin, and that magnificent feeling of blood being pulled from my veins overtook me.

"Yessss," I hissed. I reached my hand back over my shoulder and gripped his hair, holding his head in place so he wouldn't stop feeding from me. "Feels so good."

My vampire didn't answer with words. Instead, he sucked and swallowed, caressed and stroked, and then, just when I was sure I'd explode from the pleasure, he pulled his mouth back and licked at my neck.

"He's all gone," he said, his voice rough with a new kind of need.

I scrambled to turn off the tap. Then I got onto my knees, gripped the side of the tub with both hands, and lowered my head and shoulders. I spread my legs and tilted my hips so that my backside was raised and spread, the invitation clear.

Wet fingers skated reverently over my crease, and then I felt Miguel's long hair tickle my legs an instant before his tongue swiped over my sensitive skin.

"Love when you do that," I said on a sigh.

"Good," he responded, his voice scratchy as sandpaper, lust having flooded him. "Because I love doing it."

Seemingly intent on proving the truth of that statement, he ate at me with renewed vigor, sucking and licking my cleft, then pushing his tongue into my hole and wiggling it inside, even biting the pale cheeks of my rear end.

All the while, I moaned and shouted and pleaded for more.

"Fuck, you're something else," he mumbled to himself as he palmed each side of my bottom and spread me wide. "Never wanted anyone like this." He rubbed his thick thumbs over my pucker. "Never felt like this." He pushed those digits into my saliva-slicked hole. "Didn't know I could."

"Ah!" I shouted at the wonderful feeling of penetration. I pushed back, grinding myself against his hands, riding his thumbs.

"Can't wait," he grunted as he lined his throbbing erection up to my needy hole. With his thumbs still inside, spreading me wide, he bumped the mushroom head of his shaft against my entrance. "Gonna feel me in your throat," he said gruffly.

Water splashed out the side of the tub as he replaced his fingers with his shaft, shoving into me hard and deep and oh so good.

"Fuck!" he groaned.

"More," I begged.

A growl was the only warning I got before I was yanked up to a kneeling position with my back pressed to Miguel's chest. He wrapped one of his meaty forearms around my neck and the other around my belly, and continued to wage his welcome assault on my hole.

We moved in concert. I slammed down as he thrust up, both of us grunting and moaning, desperately chasing our orgasms. Miguel pinched my nipples and moved his hand up to my face, tracing my lips with his fingers before shoving two of them into my mouth and mimicking the motion of his hips.

I sucked with gusto, fellating those fingers like they were the penis that was, at that moment, doing its level best to rip me apart in the best way possible. And yet, it wasn't enough. I needed more. And Miguel seemed to know exactly how to give it to me.

He pressed his thumb to my chin and hooked the two fingers in my mouth against my cheek, tugging until my head tilted to the side. I shivered at the knowledge of what was coming next.

His fangs sank into my neck, and I screamed around the fingers that were, once again, thrusting in and out of my mouth. Miguel's testicles banged against my backside as he somehow managed to push his thick pole even deeper into my body.

The pleasure was all-consuming and I burst—white, creamy seed shot out of my untouched prick. My mate followed me over the edge, stilling and holding me tight as he came deep inside me.

"WE'LL be safe in here?" I asked nervously as I looked around the dingy room. The space was empty save for a mattress on the floor, which seemed to be the decorating style in this particular warehouse-turned-vampire-den. "Nobody's going to come back today to use it?" My question didn't make sense. It was daylight, which meant the only vampires we'd see in the warehouse were the ones already inside, two of whom were just barely out of death's grip and the other two who were friends of a sort.

"I'll keep you safe, baby." Miguel dropped our bags in the corner, wrapped his strong arms around my chest, and pulled me flush against him. "I promise." He nibbled on my earlobe. "The men who used this room aren't coming back here or going anywhere else ever again. I made sure of it." He paused and took in a deep breath, squeezing me tightly. "And I'll do the same to anybody who tries to keep us apart."

I nodded and rubbed my hands over his forearms. "I knew you'd come back for me," I whispered. "Felt it deep in my gut."

"Good," he said, his voice just as low as mine. "I'm glad. Because that's something you can always count on."

We stood together, swaying just a tad and enjoying the feeling of each other's heat, the scent of each other's body, the sound of each other's breathing...until the sound of footsteps rent the air. I stiffened and Miguel rubbed my belly, instantly soothing me.

"Miguel," Katherine called out. "I'm heading your way, so make sure you're not in some indecent position that'll leave me scarred for life."

"We'd better get dressed," Miguel said resignedly. He dug through our bags and pulled out my shorts and shirt. "Here you go," he said, holding them out to me. "I know you must be sick of wearing these. Just as soon as we get to our house, we'll buy you some new things."

"It's okay." I shrugged into my shirt. "I don't need much." It wasn't as if I'd had a huge wardrobe at my parents' den, and the things I did have were mostly hand-me-downs my mother had hemmed and shortened so they'd fit. Heck, the shorts I was wearing were full of holes and practically coming apart at the seams. It wasn't like I minded.

I'd just pulled my shorts up past my hips when Miguel stepped up to me, already fully dressed. He cupped my prick with one hand and tugged the zipper up with the other. Then he gave me a squeeze and pulled his hand out of my shorts before fastening the button.

"There," he said. "You're all set."

My skin felt hot and my breath came out in fast pants. Lord, but did that man do it for me. Just those simple touches and I was ready to tangle with him between the sheets yet again. Based on the self-satisfied smirk on my mate's face, I reckoned he knew it too.

A knock sounded at the door.

"Come on in, Katie," Miguel said over his shoulder. He didn't move his wicked gaze from me.

"Oh, good," Katherine said, sounding relieved. "I was sure I'd walk in here and find you in flagrante."

Miguel chuckled and turned to her as he wrapped an arm around my waist. "Don't worry, sweetheart," he said. "I know man parts make you queasy."

My muscles spasmed and I growled low in my throat when he called her sweetheart. I instinctively moved my body in front of his and bared my teeth at this new, albeit petite, threat.

"Oh, for Christ's sake!" Katherine shouted as she threw her arms in the air. "You"—she pointed at me—"stand down. Your man's right. I'm a girl's girl, if you know what I mean." She moved her finger up so it pointed at Miguel. "And you," she said. "I'm a professional. You've seen me heal dozens of men over the years, yourself included. Just because I don't lust after your *man parts*, as you so charmingly call them, doesn't mean I find them offensive. I just wasn't interested in a live sex show starring my uncle."

I snapped my head to the side and looked up at Miguel in surprise. "You're her uncle?" I said. "But I thought you told me you only had a nephew and he..." I let the sentence trail off, not wanting to speak of his kin's death.

"You're right," Miguel said. "Katie is using the term 'uncle' as a sign of respect."

"I would've described it more like using the term loosely," she corrected him with a wink and then she looked at me. "Miguel's nephew had a daughter, and she was..." She paused and swallowed thickly, her eyes suddenly looking a tad wet. "Sheila was my great love." Katherine closed her eyes and shook her head, causing her blonde locks to move to and fro. When she opened her eyes, they were dry and she seemed happy once again. "Sheila called this big lug Uncle Miguel, so that's how I've always known him."

My heart ached for her loss. I eased myself back against my mate, needing to feel his presence. He immediately circled both arms around me and held me close.

"What happened to Sheila?" I asked and then clamped my mouth shut, wondering if I was poking around where I had no business being.

"We came across a few men who had trouble understanding the meaning of the word no," Katherine said, anger flashing in her eyes. "We didn't go down without a fight. Especially Sheila. She was magnificent. But they were bigger than us, stronger. And there were three of them." She took in a deep breath and shrugged. "They didn't get what they wanted in the end anyway, just left us for dead. That's when Miguel got there. It was too late for Sheila, but he was able to save me."

Small as she was, with that blonde hair and those baby blue eyes, Katherine could have passed for an angel. That was, unless you heard her cuss like a sailor. "And then he made sure those pieces of shit never fucked with another woman again." She looked at me with a wicked gleam in her eyes. "I was still healing from what they did to me and from being turned, but Uncle Miguel let me watch." She sneered. "In the end, those big, strong men begged for their mamas and the Lord and anybody who'd listen. They offered to give me anything if I'd only just make him stop." She paused and almost took my breath away with the intensity of her stare. "And do you know what I told them?" she asked.

I gulped. "What?"

"I told them I wanted my Sheila back. And unless they could give me that, I was going to enjoy the show for as long as it lasted."

CHAPTER 21

"Uh, Miguel," I whispered when Katherine had left the room to gather her medical supplies.

I was sitting on the mattress cross-legged, and he was unbuttoning the shirt he'd just put on because his niece insisted that she had to coat his wounds in a special salve she'd made. He'd already dropped his drawers.

"Yeah?"

"Your, ah, niece is a little, um, intense, isn't she?"

He chuckled. "Katie is scary as fuck and smart as a whip. Nobody messes with my girl."

"Your girl?" I asked in a broken voice.

My mate's warm brown eyes settled on me and he tilted his mouth up in a crooked grin. "Oh, come on, now. You know what I mean." He squatted down in front of me, his shirt hanging open, exposing his muscular chest, and took my hands in his, then rested them on his thigh next to his thick, mouthwatering shaft. "Katie grew up next door to my nephew. I've known her since she was knee-high. And she was the first person I turned, making her one of only two, with Ted being the other." He shrugged. "She's my girl. But, Ethan." He looked deep into my eyes. "What I feel for her after several hundred years can't touch what I feel for you after a couple of weeks. I know you have one hell of a jealous and possessive streak in you." He paused and grinned. "And truth be told, I like it. But, baby, you have nothing to worry about when it comes to my loyalty and affection. I am *all* yours."

"Show me," I said, my voice husky and gritty, barely like my own.

He reached for my shorts in a flash, tugged the button open, pulled the zipper down, and fished my rapidly expanding flesh out. Then he rolled onto his back on the floor and took me with him. He spread his legs so I could settle between them and kept my hard prick in his hand, stroking it with the same desperation I felt.

"Can you reach the cream?" he asked.

I moaned and closed my eyes as I humped his hand.

"Ethan, baby." Miguel stretched his mouth up and nipped at my throat. "Your dick is the same size as your arm. Get the cream. It's right behind you, next to the bag."

The feeling of his long fingers around me was incredible, and all I could think about was his warm touch making me feel so good, so right.

"Damn, baby, come on, now." He planted his feet on the floor and canted his hips up. Then he moved his hand, and my shaft with it, until my crown touched his pucker.

"Ah!" I cried out in need, wanting to get inside that tight hole more than I'd ever wanted anything.

"There we go," he said with a chuckle. "Now that I have your attention, reach over there and get the cream."

I twisted my still clothed body and stretched over to the pile of items on the floor, feverishly pushing everything aside until I had the container of cream in my grasp. I knelt between my mate's knees and worked off the lid with shaking hands before scooping a generous portion onto my fingers and then reaching for the nude body in front of me.

"Mmm, that's it," Miguel moaned when I coated his wrinkled flesh and then pushed my slick finger inside. He moved his hand up and swiped some cream off mine and then spread it on my throbbing erection.

"Ungh," I moaned. "Oh, Lord, I can't..." I gulped. "I..."

He brushed my hand aside and pulled me forward by my prick, not stopping until I pressed against his entrance. Then he wrapped his long legs around me and propped his heels on my backside, pressing down and forcing my erection into his body.

"Miguel!" I cried.

"That's it," he whispered. "Love how you feel inside me." I bottomed out and we both gasped for air, the pleasure nearly overwhelming in its intensity. "Damn, never would have thought I'd like it this much," he said. "But with you, I do."

I planted my hands on either side of his neck and gazed into his eyes as I pulled back slowly and then shoved back in fast and hard.

"Fuck!" he shouted as he arched his back. "Again, just like that. Do it again."

So I did. Sweat dripped from my temples as I set a

punishing pace, moving faster than ever before, slamming into my mate's body over and over again.

"Ah, ah, ah," I grunted frantically, knowing I couldn't hold back much longer.

Miguel curled his hand around the back of my head and yanked me down for a bruising kiss. I felt his hand make its way between our bellies, felt him wrap it around his hard flesh and start to yank up and down. And then he pushed my head to the side, sank his fangs into my neck, and drew out my blood, sending me into a soaring orgasm that caused my vision to go dark and my throat to go hoarse from the power of my cries.

"Wow, so you were telling the truth in that letter you sent me," Katherine said. "You really are feeding from a shifter."

Miguel pulled his mouth back and yanked my shirt down so it covered my bare backside right quick. I was still buried inside him, the mating knot keeping me there. He quickly lapped at my neck and then turned his head to face the doorway.

"Katie!" he shouted. "For fuck's sake! Haven't you ever heard of knocking?"

"The door was open, so knocking wouldn't have made a lot of sense." She walked over to the mattress and plopped down. "Plus, as loud as you were, I seriously doubt you would have heard me." She cocked her chin in my direction.

"I mean, you didn't even have the presence of mind to take off his clothes. Tsk, tsk, tsk. Why rush a good thing?"

She opened her bag, looked through it, and eventually pulled out a pad of paper and a pencil. "All right, let's get down to business. Does it hurt after you feed?" she asked Miguel, her pad propped on her knee and her pencil at the ready. "How many times have you done it?" My jaw dropped open in shock at her choice of timing for this conversation. "Do you have to take in a certain amount of human blood in between?"

"He only feeds from me!" I shouted, forgetting for a moment that I had my pecker shoved up inside my nude mate and wanting to make clear that he'd never again be drinking from another.

Miguel combed his fingers through my hair in a comforting gesture. "Seriously, Katie. Get the fuck out so I can put some clothes on, and then we can finish this inquisition."

"Who's stopping you? Get dressed. I know you're a man," she said with a smirk on her face. "But I'm pretty sure you can talk and put your pants on at the same time. That's not an overwhelming amount of multitasking, is it?"

"I'm sorry, baby," Miguel said to me and then kissed my forehead. "She's crazy, but she means well."

"Hey!" Katie said in what I was pretty sure was mock offense. "You're the one who sent me a letter asking for help with your shifter's blood issue. And, seriously, I know I was joking around before, but this is an awkward way to have a conversation. Can you at least get out from under the man and put some pants on?"

"We can't separate yet, so how about you go run a couple of laps or bang your head against the wall or something to occupy yourself and we'll call you when we're done," Miguel said.

She furrowed her brow. "What do you mean you can't separate yet? Despite a lack of personal experience of the carnal sort, I'm very familiar with how the male body works, and I'm pretty sure it's just another version of what goes in must come out."

"I cannot believe I am having this conversation," Miguel said in frustration.

"I think we're good now," I whispered to him as I wiggled and worked my prick out of his body. "Everything's, uh, gone down."

"That was fast," he said.

"Are you referring to your stamina?" Katie asked. "Because that would be really, really hilarious."

"You are going to be wearing a pine overcoat if you can't keep your mouth shut," Miguel barked. "Either get out or turn your head so I can get up and get dressed."

"What, now you're shy all of a sudden? I've seen you naked before."

I growled low in my throat.

"Girl, I am going to end you!" he yelled at her.

"Oh, you're no fun," Katie said. "Fine." She twisted around so she faced the wall. "So did I hear your wolf right?" she said, sounding more serious, nervous even. "Did he say you'd taken him as your chosen?"

Miguel paused with his pants halfway up his thighs. "Yeah," he said. "You heard right."

"Your chosen?" I asked.

He sighed deeply and put his pants to rights before coming over and sitting next to me. "Chosen blood donor," he said. "It's what a vampire calls a human who he chooses to be his exclusive food source."

"I've never heard of it happening with a shifter," Katie said. "It's rare even with humans, and from what I've heard, very, very dangerous. Are you... Hey, can I turn around now? We're having a life and death conversation here, and I'm talking to a wall."

"Yeah, go ahead," Miguel answered.

"Life and death?" I asked at the same time.

"Not for you, baby," Miguel said to me as he pulled me onto his lap. "You're safe."

"That's not a promise you can make him," Katie said. "Based on my research, I know that it's very common for a vampire who takes a chosen to drain them too often, make them too weak, and then the human ends up dying and ending the vampire's life-thread right along with him."

My stomach dropped. "Is that true?" I asked in horror.

Miguel sighed. "Yes, it's true, but not for you."

"How can you promise that?" Katie shouted.

"Because I've seen how chosens react after being drained!" Miguel yelled. "I've seen them get so weak they can't leave the bed for days on end and then, eventually"—

Miguel's voice broke—"they don't leave the bed at all."

"That's what I'm saying, Uncle Miguel." Katie lowered her voice in reaction to Miguel's show of emotion. "It's rare for chosens to live long, and then the vampire perishes with them. If you keep feeding just from him, you'll bond and then you'll be limited to his blood, and when he gets weak—"

"You think I'd be doing this if I thought it would hurt Ethan?" Miguel asked in disgust. "He's different; Ethan acts nothing like my mother!" Miguel shouted.

Well, all right, then. I had to admit that I hadn't seen that one coming. And based on Katie's gaping fish impression, I got the sense she hadn't either.

"Your mother was a chosen?" she asked in shock.

Miguel petted my hair with one hand and stroked my neck with the other; the action seemed to calm him. "Yes," he said quietly. "She was my father's chosen."

Katie lost all the color in her face. "But...how?"

"What do you mean how? They were married, had three kids, he was turned, and she wanted to be his chosen."

We sat in silence while Katie processed what Miguel done told her. I was doing the same, thinking back to what little I knew about his family and then to what he'd just said.

"Miguel?" I asked quietly.

"Yeah, baby?"

"You told me your family died." I swallowed nervously, fearful I'd upset my mate by prying, but needing to understand what Katie meant when she said I could end Miguel's life-thread, that drinking only from me could make him perish.

"What happened to them?"

He didn't answer for a fair bit, just sat quietly and stroked my skin. I waited patiently, knowing he'd answer in time.

"My mother wasn't like you," he said eventually. "She had trouble keeping up with my father's need for blood, so she was weak all the time, tired. Eventually, they realized he couldn't keep taking from her without killing her, but by then it was too late for him to hunt outside the house. She'd been his chosen for years, and they'd bonded." He paused. "So he started feeding from us."

Katie's hand flew over her mouth and she gasped.

"Turns out a bonded vampire can drink from a chosen's family member." Miguel chuckled darkly and landed his pain-filled gaze on Katie. "Did you know that? Is that something you learned through your research? Except it isn't exactly the same, not quite as sustaining. So the vampire keeps drinking more and more. And because he already bonded with one chosen, he can't bond his life-thread to another, which means they keep getting weaker, until—"

"He killed them," Katie said in horror.

"One of them, yeah." Miguel nodded. "He hadn't fed from my younger sister, Maricela. She was too young. So he would alternate between my mother, my older sister, and me. Until my sister died. Then it was just my mother and me, and we both kept getting weaker until one day I passed out when he was feeding, and when I woke again, I'd been turned and they were dead. Maricela said he turned me, waited to make sure I was alive, and then walked into the sun. When he died, my mother passed too."

Katie seemed to be struck mute after that story, which was really saying something because even the sight of Miguel and I going at it hadn't stopped her from running at the mouth.

I turned in my mate's lap until I was straddling him and then I wrapped my legs around his waist and my arms around his neck. "I'm so sorry, Miguel," I whispered in his ear.

"It was a long time ago. I'm over it," he said, but the slight hitch in his voice and the way he held me just a bit too tight told me different.

"I love you," I whispered in his ear.

He choked back a cry and cupped the back of my head, pulling me so close that air couldn't pass between us. "I love you too," he said. "And you have to know that I'd walk outside at high noon before I'd let anything happen to you. Your reaction to feeding is different. If you got weak, I wouldn't do it. But you don't. After I drink from you, you're—"

"I'm stronger. I know," I said. "My body makes enough blood for both of us. I'm not worried about you hurting me. But I need to understand what she meant about life-threads because, Miguel"—I pulled my head back so I could look into his eyes—"I don't want to hurt you either."

"Oh, thank fuck, someone is finally listening to reason," Katie said. "Did you hear that, Uncle Miguel? Even your wolf knows it's a bad idea to tie your life-thread to someone who isn't immortal. He won't live forever, and if you bond with him, you won't either."

I looked at Miguel and hoped with everything I had and everything I was that he'd tell her she was wrong. But he didn't.

"You're right. I won't," he said calmly. "And that's okay."

I was sure I'd throw up. "We'll stop," I told him. "You don't have to feed only from me. I...I can handle it. We'll just—"

Miguel cupped my cheeks in both hands and gazed into my eyes. "We're not stopping anything, Ethan. We're true mates, remember? That means I'm the only one for you and you're the only one for me."

"But it'll kill you," I sobbed.

"I'll start aging, so, eventually, yeah, it probably will." He shrugged nonchalantly. "But in life we take the good with the bad. I've lived for four hundred years, and spent almost every one of them feeling lonely and hungry and cold, deep down. But you changed all that. When I'm with you, when I feed from you, I feel warm and full and right. I won't give that up."

"You can still feed from me," I said frantically. "Just feed from others too, so we don't bond like Katie said. Then you'll live forever."

"No." Miguel shook his head. "Baby, I am not feeding from anybody but you until forever comes. If we don't bond, you'll pass and I'll be left here without you. I've done that, and it isn't living. I know you're scared, but listen to me, Ethan. Bonding to a chosen isn't always a bad thing. If it's a good match, the chosen and the vampire take on each other's traits, so the human will live longer and, yes, the vampire will age where he didn't before, but he'll also be able to walk in the sun."

I thought about what he said, really thought about it, and knew I'd make the same decision if I were in his place. I'd give up anything if it meant more time with my mate. And I wondered whether I was already starting to take on some of his traits: I was stronger; I could see in the dark; I could hear better than ever before. And, anyway, shifters who lost their true mates always perished right soon after. Miguel was a vampire, not a shifter, sure enough, but he was still my true mate, so wouldn't that mean he'd die when I did, vampire-chosen bond or not?

"Okay," I said. "Thank you."

He tugged me forward until I leaned my forehead on his. "Thank you, Ethan, for making my time on this earth actually feel like living."

"You'd give up eternity just to have a few extra years with him?" Katie asked in disbelief.

Miguel sighed deeply. "It might be more than a few. It could be an extra lifetime or more. But even if that's all it is..." Miguel turned his head toward her. "Are you telling me you wouldn't do the same if it meant you could be with Sheila again?"

Katie's mouth dropped open but no words came out. "I understand," she finally said and wiped the back of her hand along her eyes. "I don't want to lose you, Uncle Miguel. You're the only family I have. But I understand." Then she climbed onto unsteady feet and started walking toward the door.

"Katie?" I said.

"Yeah?" she answered without turning around.

"I know we've just met, but I miss my family too. Maybe we can be there for each other."

"That'd be nice," she answered, her voice hoarse with tears. "I'm going to get some rest. I'll see you both at sunset."

I dropped my head onto Miguel's shoulder and thought about everything that had happened that day.

"Longest damn day of my life," he said, showing me he'd been doing the same. "The sun is going down in a few hours and we have a long drive ahead of us. How about we climb into bed and get some rest?"

"Okay," I said and reluctantly moved off his lap.

He got to his feet and put his hand on my lower back, seemingly having the same desire to maintain contact, and we walked over to the mattress.

Miguel dropped his pants to the ground as I shucked my shirt. Then he lay down and pulled me on top of him, pushed his hands down the back of my shorts, and shoved them past my hips to my ankles. I kicked them off and then snuggled on my mate's warm chest, enjoying the feeling of his skin against mine and the realization that I'd have this for the rest of my life.

"Until forever comes?" I asked him.

He kissed the top of my head and rubbed his big hand over my back. "Even longer if I can manage it," he said.

I smiled and closed my eyes, feeling safe and content as I fell asleep in my true mate's arms.

EPILOGUE

"You awake?" I whispered quietly, not wanting to wake my mate unless he was already up. "Miguel? Are you sleeping?" Okay, so maybe I wanted to wake him up just a teensy bit.

A long arm flopped backward from the warm body in front me, and a large hand landed smack dab on my backside, giving me a hard squeeze. "I am now." Miguel's just-woke-up voice was a mite scratchier and deeper than his regular voice, and it made my breath catch in my throat and my prick throb with need.

I flattened my chest to his back and ground my erection against him. "Sorry," I said. "Go back to sleep. I didn't mean to wake you."

"Ah!" I cried out when I was suddenly flipped onto my back by my sexy vampire.

In one fell swoop, he somehow managed to straddle my hips, sit on my thighs, and pin my arms over my head by crossing my hands at the wrists and holding them with one of his big hands. Of course, that left his other hand free.

"You didn't mean to wake me, huh?"

He looked positively wicked. His long black hair flowed downward over his shoulders. His chocolate eyes raked down my body like I was dinner. And he pinched my nipples, skimmed my belly, and then wrapped his hand around my aching shaft.

"Just like you didn't mean to wake me, what was it"—he glanced at the clock on our nightstand and then returned his attention to me—"two hours ago? But then, 'cause we were both conveniently awake, you shoved that big monster of yours up my ass and rode me hard until I fell asleep?"

I would have answered, or at least tried to, but I was blushing and stammering, and then he started moving his hand up and down my hard flesh and I stopped breathing.

"Or maybe it was like how you didn't mean to wake me up the time before that? But then, since I was up and you were hungry, you figured there was a convenient way to get protein without leaving the bed?"

"I didn't say that!"

"Sorry," he said, not looking the least bit sorry. "I guess I got confused after the way you devoured my dick." He smirked.

"I didn't hear you complaining," I mumbled.

He squeezed my shaft and skimmed his thumb over my crown, making me shiver and gasp.

"Oh, I'm not complaining, baby. I love the things you do to me with your mouth. I was just taking an inventory of all the ways we've tried, without any long-term success, to get you tired enough to sleep so we can figure out what to try next." He wedged his knee between my thighs, making me spread my legs wide, and then dragged one finger across my shaft, over my testicles, and down into my crease. "Do you have any ideas?"

"Not a one," I said.

He pushed his finger inside me and crooked it just right, touching that spot inside that made me moan. "Are you sure?" he asked as he pulled his finger out and then slipped it back in, manipulating my gland again.

"Yeah," I said hoarsely. "I'm sure."

Miguel released my wrists, then reached over to the nightstand, grabbed the lube, and drizzled it into my cleft so it dripped down to my hole. He pulled his finger out and rubbed it through the lube, then pushed it just inside my opening.

"Because I might have something we can try," he said. Then he shoved three slick digits into my body.

"Ah!" I cried out and ground my hips onto his hand, riding his fingers.

With his fingers in place, filling my body and tapping at my prostate, he settled down on top of me, his face hovering just above me, combing through my hair with his free hand. "That feel good, wolf?" he asked.

After nearly twenty years together, he already knew the answer. He knew what I liked, knew where to touch, where to lick, where to kiss, and where to bite. My vampire had played my body like a fiddle every day of our long lives together, and I never stopped being grateful.

"Uh-huh," I said. "Always feels good with you."

He pulled his fingers out and lined up his hard length.

Soft lips pressed to mine. "I love you, Ethan," he said tenderly, and then he pushed in hard and fast, impaling me on his thick pole over and over again.

"Miguel!" I cried out and clasped his back, scratching my nails into his skin as I grappled for purchase.

"Right here, baby," he grunted as he pounded into me. "Right fucking here."

He tangled his fingers in my hair and locked my head in place. Then he struck, sinking his fangs into me and drawing out my blood. I cried out his name and filled the space between us with my release. Miguel followed me seconds later, arching his neck and bellowing in ecstasy as he came deep inside me.

We stayed tangled together, catching our breaths, letting our hearts slow to normal, and exchanging soft licks and kisses. Eventually, Miguel rolled onto his back and pulled me close to him. I flung my leg over his hip and my arm over his chest. He tucked my head under his chin, and I sighed in contentment, pleased that my body fit just right with my mate's.

"You feel better, baby?" he asked.

"Yeah."

"You know, this visit from your family is going to be just fine. Every year you stress and fret, and then everyone has a wonderful time and you realize it was all for nothing."

"I know I'm being silly," I admitted. "It's just that Crissy's boys are already grown, starting their own families, and the twins are sure to follow suit." I shrugged. "This might be the last summer they come with Crissy for her annual trip."

"Each of your nephews brings his brood up here at least once a year. Those boys love the lake. And Joan and Leah think their godfather hung the moon. Do you really think they'll stop coming to see you?"

I licked his skin, just because I could.

"No," I conceded. "I know they'll come. And they're *our* goddaughters."

"Good, then it's settled. *Our* goddaughters are going to have a ball visiting their favorite uncles. And we'll go to Kfarkattan for a few days in the winter and rent a room in that new hotel so we can meet that Jeremy person Joan's been dating—"

"Leah," I corrected him.

"What?"

"Leah is dating Jeremiah. Has been since fall. Crissy suspects Joan's dating someone too, but she hasn't brought him around yet."

"Okay," Miguel said with a chuckle. "I stand corrected. We'll go to Kfarkattan and meet Leah's new guy. Is that better?"

I grunted.

"It's almost sunset, baby. Let's try to get some sleep."

"All right," I said and closed my eyes.

"And Ethan?"

"Yeah?"

"If you're having trouble sleeping again," he said as he skimmed his hand down my back and over to my bottom and gave me a squeeze, "you go right ahead and wake me up."

"HEY, what are you doing out here all alone?" I asked my sister as I approached. She was standing in front of the lake, looking over the water with her arms crossed over her chest and a pained expression on her face.

"I was just thinking," she said and turned to me, holding her arms wide open.

I stepped into her embrace and hugged her tightly. "I miss you more than you know, Crissy," I said.

"Oh, I know," she answered with a sniffle. "Because I miss you just as much."

We stayed together for several long minutes, neither of us wanting to let go.

"Mama and Pop are doing well?" I asked her.

She patted my shoulder and stepped back. "They're fine. Getting older. You know how it is." One corner of her mouth turned up in a wry grin. "I take that back," she said. "You don't know how it is."

I chuckled. "I'm getting older. It just doesn't show as quick on me."

"Lucky you," she said, sounding unaccountably sad.

I held up the sweater I'd picked up for her on my way out of the cottage and draped it over her shoulders. "What's going on, Crissy?" I asked, feeling more than a little concerned.

"We're fixin' to lose Joan," she said.

I jerked in shock. Of all my nieces and nephews, Joan was the most special, probably because she was the spitting image of my sister. And I didn't only mean that she looked like Crissy on the surface, though she did. But it was more than that. She had Crissy's spirit and strength. And the last couple of times I'd seen her, I noticed her eyes clouding over like Crissy's used to when she saw more than what was in front of her. I'd asked my sister about it once. She was real proud and told me her girl had inherited her gift.

"What do you mean you're going to lose Joan?"

"She's seeing someone," Crissy said. "I done told you that, right?"

"Yes." I nodded. "You did."

"Well, she hasn't brought him 'round none, but the other night we scented him on her clothes." She swallowed thickly. "He's human."

It was a shocking revelation, sure enough. Humans and shifters didn't mix. But neither did shifters and vampires, so our family was particularly well suited to overlook such things.

"She's young, Crissy," I reminded my sister. "Barely twenty. Maybe she just needs time to explore."

"Maybe." My sister nodded. "But Richie done told her she'd have to move out if he ever smelled the human on her again."

My jaw dropped. "Richie said that?"

Crissy gave me a sad smile. "Don't look so surprised,

little brother. She's his baby girl, and he don't want to give her to no man. Finding out this one's a human is probably just an excuse, but he won't listen to reason. He thinks he can tell her what to do, that she'll choose her daddy over her man. He can't seem to see that she's grown and he's pushing her away."

"What are you going to do?" I asked.

"I'm going to do the only thing I can. I'm going to let her go." Crissy looked back at the lake and rubbed her hands over her arms. "It ain't easy being a female. We have to be strong, just like the males, but our strength needs to be quieter, steadier, more constant. We bring children into the world, through our bodies, through our love. And it's our responsibility to feed them, nurture them, and protect them so they're able to make their way long after we're gone. I raised my girl the best way I knew how, and now I have to trust her to do what's right. Even iffen it ain't under my watch."

I draped my arm over my sister's shoulders and absorbed what she'd told me. Talking to Richie wouldn't do no good. First off, it sounded like he'd already dug his heels in nice and deep. And besides, maybe it was time for Joan to move out of her parents' den and gain a little independence. I'd run off with Miguel when I was the same age as my niece and it was the best thing I'd ever done.

"Do you want me to have Miguel talk to her?" I asked my sister. "You know she's crazy about him. He's probably the only person around who can pry into her life without getting his neck chopped off."

Crissy snickered. "He is, at that. Can't say I rightly blame her." She smirked at me. "We've all seen your man, and I didn't raise no fools."

Well, I couldn't argue with that.

I WAVED goodbye to my family as they drove away, and then turned back to our cottage and started laughing.

"What are you doing?" I asked Miguel.

"Enjoying the sunlight," he said.

As time passed, we'd noticed his tolerance for the sun was building up. He still couldn't walk outside in broad daylight. But during times like this, when the sun was halfway down and the sky was awash in pinks and oranges, we could sit together on our covered porch and enjoy the evening air. And it looked like that was just what my mate was fixing to do, seeing as how he was stripping off his clothes until he was naked as the day he was born.

I walked over to him and took my spot by his side on our new porch swing. "Aren't you cold?" I asked.

He reached down and came up with a thick blanket. "I've got it covered, baby." He wrapped the soft cotton around both of our shoulders and then curled his arm around me and pulled me tight against him. I smiled up at my mate before resting my head on his shoulder.

"Did you have a good time visiting with everyone?"

he asked while he squeezed my knee and then caressed my thigh.

"I did, at that," I answered. "You were right, as usual. Everyone had fun." I moved my hand over to his belly and traced each of his tight muscles. "Did you have a chance to talk to Joan before they left?" I asked him.

"Yeah, I did. Just for a few minutes."

I tilted my chin up and looked at him. "And? What'd she say about this man she's seeing and about moving out of her daddy's den?"

"Not much," he answered. "She pretty much told me the same things you heard from Crissy."

"Was she upset?" I asked.

"No." Miguel shook his head. "Actually, she seemed really at peace, more than I've ever noticed before."

I sighed. "Well, I suppose that's good, then."

"Yeah, it is. She did say one thing that was sort of strange."

"What's that?" I asked.

"She said she's going to need our help with something really important, but she wouldn't tell me what it was, just said we'd know when the time came. And then she got that weird look in her eyes, you know, like the one Crissy used to get, and she said I should tell you that it was worth it and that she was happy."

"Huh," I said, not really knowing what to make of that, but accustomed to it after growing up with Crissy. "Well, I reckon happy is good."

Miguel shifted a bit and wrapped his long fingers around my neck, pushing my chin up so our gazes met. "You know what would make me happy right now?" he asked, his husky voice giving me a good indication of what he was fixing to say.

"What's that?" I asked.

"Watching you strip out of those clothes and sit on my lap." He planted his feet on the wood floor and pushed back, making us rock. "I think we can have a lot of fun on this swing."

I'd never taken my clothes off faster in my life. My very long, very blessed life.

THE END

REVIEWS

Johnnie: Like always the sex was deliciously hot and steamy, yet still sweet (CC does that SO well) and the ending was satisfyingly sigh worthy.

— Sinfully Sexy

Jumping In: It was delicious, beautiful, hot and sexy and lots and lots of other words that just wouldn't do it justice.

— Archaeolibrarian

Blue Mountain: This is a fabulous audio book, one that I will listen to again and again. A keeper. Go and grab your copy.

— Love Bites Silk Ties

Where He Ends and I Begin: It is also sexy and smutty, and filled with a very large amount of dirty fun.

— Prism Book Alliance

The One Who Saves Me: This story is so intense, and Cardeno C.'s amazing storytelling keeps you going until the end, when all is explained.

— The Novel Approach

McFarland's Farm: A wonderful novella full of emotion, acceptance and love.

— Gay Listed Book Reviews

ABOUT THE AUTHOR

Cardeno C.—CC to friends—is a hopeless romantic who wants to add a lot of happiness and a few *awwws* into a reader's day. Writing is a nice break from real life as a corporate type and volunteer work with gay rights organizations. Cardeno's stories range from sweet to intense, contemporary to paranormal, long to short, but they always include strong relationships and walks into the happily-ever-after sunset.

Email: cardenoc@gmail.com

Website: www.cardenoc.com

Twitter: https://twitter.com/cardenoc

Facebook: http://www.facebook.com/CardenoC

Pinterest: http://www.pinterest.com/cardenoC

Blog: http://caferisque.blogspot.com

OTHER BOOKS BY CARDENO C.

SIPHON
Johnnie

HOPE
McFarland's Farm
Jesse's Diner

PACK
Blue Mountain
Red River

HOME
He Completes Me
Home Again
Just What the Truth Is
Love at First Sight
The One Who Saves Me
Where He Ends and I Begin
Walk With Me

FAMILY
The Half of Us
Something in the Way He Needs
Strong Enough
More Than Everything

MATES
In Your Eyes
Until Forever Comes
Wake Me Up Inside

NOVELS
Strange Bedfellows
Perfect Imperfections
Control *(with Mary Calmes)*

NOVELLAS
A Shot at Forgiveness
All of Me
Places in Time
In Another Life & Eight Days
Jumping In

AVAILABLE NOW

Wake Me Up Inside

(A Mates Story)

A powerful Alpha wolf shifter and a strong-willed human overcome traditions ingrained over generations and uncover long-buried secrets to fulfill their destiny as true mates.

Regarded as the strongest wolf shifter in generations, Alpha Zev Hassick is surprised and confused by his attraction to his best friend. His very human, very male best friend. A male shifter has to mate with a female shifter to keep his humanity, so shifters can't be gay. Yet, everything inside Zev tells him Jonah is his true mate.

Maintaining a relationship with the man he has loved since childhood isn't easy for Jonah Marvel, but he won't let distance or Zev's odd family get in their way. When unexplained ailments begin to plague Jonah, he needs to save his own life and sanity in order to have a future with Zev.

Zev and Jonah know they're destined for each other, but they must overcome traditions ingrained over generations and long-buried secrets to fulfill their destiny.

In Your Eyes

(A Mates Story)

Two very different men with a tumultuous history must overcome challenges from all sides and see past their society's rules to realize they are destined for one another.

Raised to become Alpha of the Yafenack pack, Samuel Goodwin dedicates his life to studying shifter laws, strengthening his body, and learning from his father. But despite his best efforts, Samuel can't relate to people, including those he's supposed to lead.

When Samuel meets Korban Keller, the son of a neighboring pack's Alpha, he reacts with emotion instead of intellect for the first time in his life. Resenting the other shifter for throwing him off-balance, Samuel first tries to intimidate Korban and then desperately avoids him. What he can't do is forget Korban's warm eyes, easy smile, and happy personality.

When a battle between their fathers ends tragically, Samuel struggles to lead his pack while Korban works to break through Samuel's emotional barriers. Two very different men with a tumultuous history must overcome challenges from all sides and see past their society's rules to realize they are destined for one another.

Johnnie

(A Siphon Story)

A Premier lion shifter, Hugh Landry dedicates his life to leading the Berk pride with strength and confidence. Hundreds of people depend on Hugh for safety, success, and happiness. And at over a century old, with more power than can be contained in one body, Hugh relies on a Siphon lion shifter to carry his excess force.

When the Siphon endangers himself and therefore the pride, Hugh must pay attention to the man who has been his silent shadow for a decade. What he learns surprises him, but what he feels astounds him even more.

Two lions, each born to serve, rely on one another to survive. After years by each other's side, they'll finally realize the depth of their potential, the joy in their passion, and a connection their kind has never known.

Blue Mountain

(A Pack Story)

Exiled by his pack as a teen, Omega wolf Simon Moorehead learns to bury his gentle nature in the interest of survival. When a hulking, rough-faced Alpha catches Simon on pack territory, he tries to escape what he's sure will be imminent death. But instead of killing him, the Alpha takes Simon home.

A man of action, Mitch Grant uproots his life to support his brother in leading the Blue Mountain pack. Mitch lives on the periphery, quietly protecting everyone, but always alone. A mate is a dream come true for Mitch, and he won't let little things like Simon's rejections, attacks, and insults get in their way. With patience, seduction, and genuine care, Mitch will ride out the storm while Simon slays his own ghosts and Mitch's loneliness.

All of Me

To bond with his destined mate, an Alpha wolf must look past what he sees and trust what he feels.

Bonded by their parents before they were conceived, wolf shifters Abel and Kai adored each other since they were children. As teens, the two future Alphas took the next step in their bonding process and vowed to remain true to one another until Kai came of age. But when tragedy struck, Abel felt betrayed and ran from Kai instead of completing their mating.

Abel never stops yearning for the man who was supposed to lead by his side, and after years without contact, Kai returns, broken and on death's door. If Abel wants to fulfill their destiny and merge their packs, he'll need to look past what he saw and trust his heart.

Strange Bedfellows

Can the billionaire son of a Democratic president build a family with the congressman son of a Republican senator? Forget politics, love makes strange bedfellows.

As the sole offspring of the Democratic United States president and his political operative wife, Trevor Moga was raised in an environment driven by the election cycle. During childhood, he fantasized about living in a made-for-television family, and as an adult, he rejected all things politics and built a highly successful career as far from his parents as possible.

Newly elected congressman Ford Hollingsworth is Republican royalty. The grandson of a revered governor and son of a respected senator, he was bred to value faith, family, and the goal of seeing a Hollingsworth in the White House.

When Trevor and Ford meet, sparks fly and a strong friendship is formed. But can the billionaire son of a Democratic president build a family with the congressman son of a Republican senator? Forget politics, love makes strange bedfellows.

Made in the USA
Middletown, DE
12 May 2020

94521108R00144